DUE DATE			

Her
Infinite
Variety

Also by Louis Auchincloss

Honorable Men
Diary of a Yuppie
Skinny Island
The Golden Calves
Fellow Passengers
The Lady of Situations
False Gods
Three Lives
Tales of Yesteryear
The Collected Stories of Louis Auchincloss
The Education of Oscar Fairfax
The Atonement and Other Stories
The Anniversary and Other Stories

NONFICTION

Reflections of a Jacobite
Pioneers and Caretakers
Motiveless Malignity
Edith Wharton
Richelieu
A Writer's Capital
Reading Henry James
Life, Law and Letters
Persons of Consequence: Queen Victoria and Her Circle
False Dawn: Women in the Age of the Sun King
The Vanderbilt Era
Love Without Wings
The Style's the Man
La Gloire: The Roman Empire of Corneille and Racine
The Man Behind the Book

Her Infinite Variety

Louis Auchincloss

Houghton Mifflin Company

Boston   New York

2000

For information about permission to reproduce selections from
this book, write to Permissions, Houghton Mifflin Company,
215 Park Avenue South, New York, New York 10003.

Library of Congress Cataloging-in-Publication Data

Auchincloss, Louis.
Her infinite variety / Louis Auchincloss.
p. cm.
ISBN 0-618-02191-4
I. Title.
PS3501.U25 H47   2000
813'.54—dc21   99-047302

Book design by Anne Chalmers
Typefaces: Monotype Walbaum and Linotype-Hell Didot

Printed in the United States of America

QUM 10 9 8 7 6 5 4 3 2 1

For

ANDREW POPE

Fine Friend and Able Agent

Age cannot wither her, nor custom stale
Her infinite variety.

— *Antony and Cleopatra*

Her
Infinite
Variety

1

VIOLET LONGCOPE had, from the earliest signs of her daughter's incipient beauty, drilled into Clarabel's lovely head the warning that a single unwary submission of the heart to the wrong male charm could throw a girl perhaps irretrievably off the smooth tracks of the best laid life plan. The warning was all the more necessary for a girl raised not only in a university town but in the very heart of a university. Pierpont in 1937 was the newest of the colleges in Yale's new college plan, and Violet's husband, Irving Longcope, was its popular master. Their residence, forming a corner of the creamy square Gothic edifice, ornamented with ugly pediments and narrow mullioned windows, was a social center for the undergraduates who came freely in and out to attend her teas or her husband's famed "readings aloud" in the vast cellar rumpus room. It had not taken any of these young men long to cultivate the acquaintance of the tall lissome blond daughter of the master, with her infectiously sympathetic laugh, her large, amused yet tantalizingly detached gray-blue eyes, her high spirits and her bold graceful stride.

She had certainly not had her looks from her mother. Not that Violet lacked attractions. She was generally considered the brightest and wittiest of the college masters' wives (not that this, as she too often reminded herself, was such a compliment), but such qualities in a woman were not those that appealed most to young men. Violet had been pretty enough as a girl, but at fifty her long thin face had sharpened; her chin was more pointed, her nose more aquiline, and her pale, rather staring eyes and way of twisting her head around to look at you while her small body remained absolutely still might suggest a bird, though a bird of sharp acuity and critical acumen. Some of the faculty wives professed to be afraid of her tongue, and she didn't mind this a bit. She would have adored to preside over a salon, and would have paid with her eyesight for Madame du Deffand's famous one. And what did she have instead? A circle of Yale students for tea and an occasional faculty supper where the men argued tediously about tenure.

And she didn't even get the right undergraduates at tea! The "prep school" crowd, the sons of her girlhood friends, the scions of old New York and New England first families — these not only shunned such sissy affairs as teas; they didn't even apply to Pierpont, but to Pierson or Davenport or Berkeley. Poor Pierpont, in the inexplicably arbitrary way of fashion, or perhaps because of one year's assignment to it of some particularly unattractive and riotous youths, had acquired the odious name of a "meatball" college. Irving was sufficiently known as an English professor to attract some of the "white shoe" crowd to his readings in the cellar — and Irving, for all his booming enthusiasm for the down-to-earth Chaucer and the yearning democracy of Walt Whitman, had a distinct preference for handsome, well-heeled men who belonged to the better fraternities and senior societies — while she had to hand out her cups and cakes to hungry bursary students, to timid rustics who regarded her teas as elegant social rituals and to epicene youths who sought a female oasis in a rather too boisterously male society.

Of her two children, only Clara had seemed moldable — at least up to the present crisis. Clara, almost from the beginning, had been the star of the little family; in Clara, and in Clara alone, had been Violet's hope of a new and brighter life. Brian, hunky and moody and truculently independent, already a junior at Yale, was absorbed in physics and had no interest in the drama of personalities that so occupied his mother. He would go his own way, God bless him, and never need her. But Clara could have the world — or could have had it — if she could only learn to want it enough! She had warmth and charm and brains and humor, and the way she wrinkled her small, upturned nose as she smiled or laughed and widened her eyes in delight was captivating to the coldest male. She was so enchanting that it sometimes seemed to Violet that she might be playing a part, like an actress in repertory who could be Imogen one night, Cleopatra the next, and, yes, even Lady Macbeth on a third.

Violet, over her husband's opposition — and she never hesitated to overrule him, sharply and effectively, in the very few matters about which she cared — had sent Clara for three years to Saint Timothy's, an exclusive girls' boarding school, to get her away from New Haven and to introduce her to the kind of women Violet thought would be helpful to her later in life, and the result had been very satisfactory. Clara had not only led the school academically; she had excelled in sports, and the leadership that she had easily established among her classmates showed that she would never be one of those foolhardy women who neglect to make firm allies in their own sex. From Saint Timothy's she had gone to Vassar, and at Vassar she had developed the unfortunate habit of coming home every weekend. Why? It was surely not for the pleasure of seeing her parents, or even her brother, of whom she was very fond. No, it could be for only one reason, and that would surely be the wrong one.

And, of course, it was Bobbie Lester. He was just the kind of young man Violet had most dreaded because he was the hardest to fault. He was Irving's principal assistant, a senior working his way through Yale as a faculty helper, not exactly one of the social crowd but "connected," as the saying is, his family being respectably impoverished, with an heroic father killed in France in 1918 and a brave little mother who gave bridge lessons to her stylish but charitable friends. Bobbie was handsome and athletic and cheerful and idealistic; his golden ambition was to return to the prep school he had so extravagantly loved, and where he had been football captain and senior prefect, and teach history and coach crew and train boys for the great adventure of life.

When a beaming Clara and Bobbie came into the garden, hand in hand, that Sunday afternoon, where Violet was sitting, with the great hulk of Irving radiating his blessings behind them, to tell her that they were now really engaged, and wanted to be married in June because Bobbie had been promised the desired job at his beloved prep school upon his graduation, Violet found that she simply could not speak. She got up, hurried into the house and locked herself in her bedroom. Nor would she open it when Clara pounded on the door and Irving thundered through the keyhole. She stayed there until she knew it was time for Clara to return to Vassar and watched her from the window as Bobbie drove her to her train. Then she emerged to face her husband.

"There's no point discussing something about which you all have made up your minds."

And she maintained her position until the following weekend when Clara returned. She arrived early on Saturday morning and went to her mother's chamber, where Violet was still in bed, drinking coffee and working on a crossword puzzle. She sat firmly down in the chair beside her.

"Mother, you *must* talk to me!"

Violet filled in a word before looking up. "You're at liberty to wreck your own life, my dear. But don't ask me to be your auxiliary. I'll have nothing to do with it!"

"But if I *beg* you to discuss it with me!"

Violet put down the paper. "In that case, of course, I will. I've been waiting for the moment when I thought you might be ready to listen. Really to listen, I mean. There's no point discussing an engagement with a person determined that nothing will convince her that her love is not the be-all and end-all of her life."

"And you think that my wanting to talk to you may mean that I'm having my doubts about that?"

"I don't really think anything, darling, except that you and I might just possibly be on the verge of a mutual communication."

Clara jumped up from her chair at this and strode to the window. How her every move was graceful! Violet knew that her daughter, no matter how keenly her emotions were aroused, never lost sight of how she appeared to observing eyes.

"It's only because your deafening silence has driven me mad!" Clara exclaimed, turning now to glare at the complacent maternal figure in the bed. "As I'm sure you meant it to!"

Violet glanced down at her discarded puzzle. "We don't have to talk at all, my dear."

"Oh, you know we do! Please, Mummie, let's get on with it. Tell me why you hate Bobbie."

"I don't hate him at all. I rather like him. As a matter of fact, if I were ten or fifteen years younger and your father not in the picture, I could fancy him as a kind of *cavaliere servente*. For a time, anyway."

"For a time! That's it, then. You don't think that as a lover — for that's what your flossy term means, I suppose — that he'd last?"

"Yes, dear. That *is* it. In the proverbial nutshell. I don't think he'd last. And I don't think he *will* last. For you, I mean."

"You mean you don't think he'd be faithful?"

"You know I don't mean that. He'll be faithful, all right. To the very end. To the bitter end. And it will be bitter, too, because he'll be too nice, too dear, too much of a sweet teddy bear, for you ever to shed. That's where he'll have you, my girl. And for life."

6

"Why should I ever want to shed him?"

"To save yourself from suffocation. Look, Clara. You've fallen in love with a pair of shining black eyes, a muscular torso with broad shoulders and sculpted thighs, an infectious enthusiasm and some highfalutin ideas — the whole glittering costume of youth — and all of it directed at you with a passionate sincerity!"

"It *is* sincere, then? You admit that?"

"Oh, totally. That's the trap that's set for us poor females. Not that we don't have our own, but that's not what I'm talking about now. The male animal only wants one thing, and he's off after he's got it. But the male human wants us for life. You'll find yourself snared in that school. *He'll* do well enough there, for the boys will like him, and the masters won't fear his competition."

"Why won't they?"

"Because they'll see he hasn't got the imagination or drive or even the backbiting ability ever to be a headmaster, unless he runs into a Mr. Chips situation, which isn't likely. And as he grows older, he will become a kind of school legend, much loved but a bit laughed at by the older and more sophisticated boys who will joke among themselves at his little clichés."

"Mother, stop! You're too awful!"

"You mean too true. Has Bobbie ever said anything that would impress you from the lips of a homely man? You know he hasn't, though you hate to face it. But face it you will when the hair begins to recede from his temples, and his fanny begins to widen, and he starts to repeat himself, or rather when you start to notice it. That's a little process called life, and there's nothing on earth you can do about it."

7

"But even if what you say is true or, let us say, has a molecule of truth in it, which I'm not for a minute conceding, there'd be things I could do with myself at the school. I wouldn't have to be submerged in Bobbie's teaching life!"

"Oh, yes, I suppose you could help in local charities. Or even tutor some of the backward boys. Or take up watercolors. And, of course, it would be an ideal life for a writer, if you had any gift in that line. But I don't see that as your cup of tea. And the atmosphere of a school community can be a terrible anaesthetic."

"I'd have children, I hope. And the support of a loving husband."

"The last you'd certainly have. And I'm sure Bobbie would be a vigorous lover. But you'd pay a high price for those wild nights, my girl. And at the risk of your calling me an old bawd, I'd like to point out that Bobbie is far from being the only male who could give them to you."

"Really, Mother, I wouldn't have thought it of you!"

"You think women my age don't have their fantasies about sex? Dream on, my dear!"

Violet had sown her seed; she knew when to stop. When Bobbie came to lunch that day, she was very cordial, particularly as he played into her hand with his theory of how to redirect the disciplinary emphasis of the school to which he was headed.

"I believe there has been too much of the negative in the moral code of the preparatory schools," he opined gravely. "Too many can'ts and don'ts. One headmaster is even reputed to have said that if his vocabulary were limited to a single word and that word was 'no,' he could still get by. I think boys are better than that. After all, they are young men. I think if you challenge them with something positive, put before them a 'do' or a 'let's go' instead of a bleak prohibition, you have a good chance of lighting the real fire inside them. It's the difference between offense and defense, between the guy with the puck before his stick and the goalie. Give the boys something really to go for . . ."

She didn't have to look at Clara. She knew that she was wincing.

Violet was very well aware that she was engaged in a struggle that she might lose, but that didn't matter to her. She wanted to be sure that she had done all she could to keep her daughter from making *her* mistake, or rather from making a much graver one. For Bobbie Lester was never going to have a career that approached the success of Irving Longcope's. Indeed, most of Violet's friends and relatives considered that she had done very well for herself. Irving was a college master and a popular teacher; he cut a sufficient figure on the Yale campus. That was all very well, and Violet was not a woman to undervalue her few blessings as she took them out, one by one, from the tight little chest of her memories and reappraisals, counted them and put them carefully back. It was all very well, truly, but Irving Longcope had not become half the man she had expected him to be.

Her family, the Edeys, had been the kind of old New Yorkers who had been somehow able to subsist, with moderate but unquestioned respectability, for generations on the fringe of Knickerbocker society, supported by the exiguous rentals of some tightly retained strips of lower

Manhattan real estate. Her father had attained an obscure fame by writing a popular book of opera plots with photographs of the great divas of the golden age — Calvé, Eames, Ternina — and some moderately witty *vers de société*. He had been a fussy old dandy, a perennially white-tied figure seated in the back of the boxes of the parterre, in one of which he actually managed to die. His wife was the constantly ailing *malade imaginaire* of the era, mild, sweet and uncomplaining, who didn't mind that her spouse was so often asked to dine out *en garçon*. Violet had been sent to Miss Chapin's School; she had grown up with all the "right" people; in fact she had grown up with none others. But she had always known that her family lived on the edge, that the morning mail contained bills that her father would crumple with a grunt of outrage and that, as a debutante, she had come out only on the coattails, as it were, of a rich second cousin, the honor of whose ball she was allowed to share. And in the New York of the century's first decade everyone knew everything about everyone else.

Irving Longcope had seemed the perfect and hardly hoped for answer to the problem of a young woman of no fortune and no very striking looks in a milieu of rather garish prosperity. In 1911 he was a handsome, stalwart figure of a man, some dozen years older than herself, with a military stature and the reputation of a hero — he had fought in Cuba and written a best seller about the charge up San Juan Hill — and he was looking for a wife, it was rumored, because he was running for Congress and the party wanted a married man. Violet's father had for once proved useful; he had met him in an opera box and taken the delighted Rough Rider backstage to introduce him to Jean de Reszke, who had sung Siegfried that night, after which it had been in order to invite him to dinner, and Violet had done the rest.

She had seen at once that for all Irving's rather intimidating bluster he was essentially shy, particularly with women, and dreaded falling into the clutches of a bossy one. He wanted a quiet and admiring spouse, and it took her only a few weeks of what he was later to describe too often as "a whirling courtship" in which he "swept her off her feet" to convince him that she would be the Mrs. Longcope of his fondest dreams.

But it was not long after their union that Violet began to realize that she had misconceived her man. He handled his campaign for Congress with every ineptitude, disregarding the advice of the bosses and speaking out on issues as if party lines didn't exist. He lost and lost badly, and it was evident that his political career was over before it had begun, and Violet's dream of the gubernatorial mansion in Albany or a high position in Washington as the wife of an Empire State senator vanished forever. Irving had some money but not enough for a family; he studied for a master's degree in English and got a job teaching at Yale. It seemed the best he could do.

He was never a deep or even an illuminating scholar or critic — Violet saw that clearly enough — but he had an enthusiasm for the manly verse of Browning, the realistic vigor of Fielding, the adventurous sagas of Conrad, the rollicking satires of Byron, that was contagious, particularly with young men more addicted to sports and parties than to academic studies, and his reputation spread. It was

Violet who kept her ear to the ground, and when the college system was established, it was she who, having quietly cultivated the friendship of President Angell and others in authority, managed to keep Irving's name in the running for a mastership.

It was not easy, for many of the faculty were against the appointment of a professor who appeared to be too lazy (Irving claimed he was busy with his *real* job: teaching) to publish scholarly works. And even after his appointment to Pierpont, the opposition became so acerbic that Irving's rowdier enthusiasts in the undergraduate body broke into the offices of the leading anti-Longcope professors to cover their desks with garbage. In the end Irving compromised with his critics, not very satisfactorily to either side, by publishing a handbook of Browning, largely a reworking of his master's dissertation.

There had been no further excitement. Indeed, there had been little further change. Irving through the years had seemed to dwindle into a voice, a large sonorous voice to be sure, delivering the identical lectures on Victorian poets and novelists to gradually less admiring undergraduates and in some cases to hostile ones converted to Eliot and Pound and Scott Fitzgerald. All of them knew they could cut his classes at will and read his well-known discourses in a trot. But he was still something of a Yale institution; everyone knew who he was. And Violet had given up asking herself what had gone wrong. Nothing had gone wrong. Irving was what he had been from the beginning: a golden windbag. The error had been hers and hers alone.

Clara did not come home again for three weeks. She

telephoned that she was studying for exams. Bobbie protested to her parents that she wouldn't let him visit her at Vassar, and Violet, who had never shown him her hand and had let him suppose that her strange conduct at the engagement announcement was mere shock, urged him not to interfere with her studies and assured him that all was well. She was even beginning to hope that it might be.

But Clara had another arrow to her bow. She appeared suddenly one Saturday morning and sought a long, private conference with her father, presumably to enlist his aid. Violet waited for them to finish, seated rather grimly in her little garden, protected from the college quadrangle by a low brick wall, her needlepoint in hand. Was it possible, she wondered, that Clara could really expect substantial help from her father?

When they came out of the house at last, they seemed girded for battle. They sat together, rather absurdly, on a bench not quite large enough to hold two.

"Our daughter tells me that you have some objections to the young man of her choice."

"You might put it that way, yes."

"And you have not seen fit to impart them to me. May I ask why?"

"Because *you* are not planning to marry him."

The ponderous graying figure before her seemed to brace itself to sustain this shock. Violet, surveying him with a cruel detachment, had never felt less married.

"That seems a new slant in the married relationship!" he exclaimed.

"Or a very old one."

Irving cleared his throat as he decided he had better return to the point. "Is it your position, Violet, that this amiable and attractive young man, equipped with an honorable character, respectable antecedents and a reasonably secure future, is not a qualified candidate for our daughter's hand?"

"I don't deny any of the attributes you ascribe to him. I have considered them carefully. And I have found them inadequate."

"Because he lacks riches?"

"Not at all."

"Or isn't blue-blooded enough for you?"

"You know that's ridiculous."

"What is it, then?"

"Simply that he will never become, by the remotest stretch of the imagination, even the hollow copy of a great man."

Irving's glance at his daughter seemed to indicate that they were dealing with one at least temporarily bereft of her senses. "So! You fly high, I see. And what leads you to suppose that Clara is entitled to — or even wants — a great man?"

"Only the fact that she is capable of getting one."

"And that is all that matters to you? Worldly success?"

"I never said it had to be worldly. But yes, it would have to be success, of a sort. Even if Clara herself were the only one to recognize it."

"What about Clara's happiness? Or doesn't that matter to you?"

"Oh, I care a great deal about Clara's happiness. More perhaps than you do."

"And just what do you mean by that?"

"That I think I know her better than you do."

"You think she's more like *you*, that's what it is, isn't it?"

"I think she's ambitious, yes."

"As you are?"

"Yes."

"Oh, Mother!" There were sudden tears in Clara's eyes.

Irving looked very grave as he now stood up. "Does that mean that she can't be happy without what *you* call success?"

"Yes!"

"And that you can't be, either?" In the silence that followed, Violet simply stared up at him. "Violet, are you trying to tell me that *you* haven't been happy?"

"Yes!"

"Oh stop it, you two, for God's sake stop it!" Clara thrust herself between them and then turned, with a despairing look, and shook her mother by the shoulders. "Will you even wreck your marriage to prove me wrong?" She broke away from her parents with a sob. "I don't know where I am anymore. I don't know what I'll do!"

Violet always knew when to stop. She signaled to her husband to leave their daughter alone and went out for a long walk. When she returned, Clara had gone back to Vassar, and Irving at lunch had the good sense not to return to the dangerous topic of what regrets, if any, his wife harbored about her quarter of a century with himself.

❖

There he was! Slipping into the back of the living room to sit by Clara on a sofa, not threading his way through the twenty-odd students who had assembled around the table where his hostess was pouring tea, though it was his first appearance at one of her little gatherings and he should properly have come over to greet her, even if he wasn't aware that Violet had been a classmate of his mother's. But the Hoyts were all that way — a rule to themselves, it used to be said. He would come with his swanky pals to Irving's readings in the cellar — these passed his muster — but to a silly tea at "meatball" Pierpont? Never! Only Clara could have changed *that*.

Violet watched him with a cautious eye — not that she need fear his noticing. He was intent in his talk with Clara. He looked as if he ought to be much handsomer than he was, which in an odd way made him so. He was tall and thin with a long narrow head and a dark complexion. His brow was high, his nose strong with a slight, quite superior hook; there was something of the red Indian about him, and indeed his mother's family, the Kanes, were supposed to have a squaw somewhere in their ancestry. Everything about Trevor Hoyt, from the easy smiling way he seemed to take over the chatter of Clara's little group, whom he probably despised, to the blackness of his well-pressed and well-fitting suit and the radiant scarlet of his wide tie proclaimed an assurance that was curiously inoffensive.

How different, Violet recalled, from his mother! Charlotte Kane, child of a Morgan partner, had been as a schoolgirl at Miss Chapin's as big and plain and bossy as Charlotte Hoyt, wife of the president of the Bank of Commerce, was at present, the only differences being that the older woman was gray and gravelly-voiced and fifty pounds heavier. But Violet did not have to read many social columns or talk to many of her old-time friends to know that Mrs. Hamilton Hoyt was a dominant voice in the New York world of the private schools, the subscription dances, the opera, the art museums, the benefit balls. When people, appalled at the rapid turnover and changing manners of the urban élite, asked if there was anything left of "old New York society," the answer was apt to be: "Well, we still have the Hamilton Hoyts."

Violet sought her daughter's eye now and, pointing to Hoyt, signaled to her to bring him over. It was the first time she had dared even to notice a beau of her daughter's since the shedding of poor Bobbie. She knew not to push her luck. Clara spoke to her friend now, and a minute later he was seated at Violet's side.

"I'm glad to meet you, Mr. Hoyt. I used to know your mother."

"Really?"

"We were at school together at Miss Chapin's."

Was there the faintest flicker of surprise in those dark eyes? Had he thought it the least bit odd that a mere spouse of academe should have been educated with the daughter of a Morgan partner? If so, his recovery was quick and natural.

"May I give her your best when I see her next?"

"Please do. The bad lady in one of Oscar Wilde's comedies says of the good one that at school she always won the good conduct prize. Well, Miss Chapin didn't hand out such a prize, but if she had, your mother would have certainly got it."

"Yes, Mother's quite something, isn't she?"

He was used to hearing his mother praised; that was not the way with him. "And she has continued to gather all the prizes, right through life, has she not? But tell me something, Mr. Hoyt. Supposing your mother had been a man . . . that is, if you can imagine such a thing."

His laugh was spontaneous. "Oh, I can easily imagine it!"

"What would she have become?"

"President, at least!"

"Like the great Theodore? I remember at school a daughter of President Roosevelt saying to your mother: 'My father calls your father a malefactor of great wealth.' And your mother snapping right back with: 'Mine calls yours an irresponsible demagogue.'"

She saw that he was delighted to have his family identified with the great. The animosity only added to the compliment. "That sounds like Mother all right. Straight to the jaw!"

"But isn't it a pity that her talents didn't have a wider scope? We poor women can only dream of the top spots in life. While you, for example — nothing stands in your way. Your only trouble will be — if you go into your father's bank — that envious people will attribute the success you owe to your own abilities to the family tie."

Oh, she had all his interest now! "That's perfectly true, Mrs. Longcope. And I've had to do some serious thinking about it. I've wondered if I shouldn't at least start somewhere else."

"And then you could shift over when you've made your mark."

"Exactly!"

"Let me see your hand." She turned over what he promptly exhibited to her and pretended to read the palm, smiling at her little joke. "You will do very well. Madame Sosostris tells you so."

"If I survive this war that Herr Hitler seems to be threatening."

"You will. You have the look of a survivor. But tell me something. Would you object to your wife's having a career?"

He became at once wary. Was she sounding him out about Clara? "Not so much if any kids we had were older and away at school. And so long as she was home in the evenings and shared vacations with me and wasn't working all the time."

"In some dreary law office or accounting firm? I can't blame you. Maybe some time in the future we women may come to that, and then we'll be as dull as you men!" Here she smiled and gave his hand a pat. "Not you, my dear Mr. Hoyt — or Trevor, if I may call you that — for I see you're not the least bit dull. And I can talk to *you*. But if you're a friend of Clara's, I wish you'd talk some sense into her."

"You mean Clara wants a career?"

"She talks of going into advertising. Do you find that attractive? To spend her life hoodwinking people into thinking they can do something about their bad breath and body odor?"

"Phew! I do not!"

"It's not the way I used to dream of her future."

"How did you see it?" He was distinctly interested now.

"I saw her as a partner to some big man. Sharing his career. As an ambassadress, for example, in diamonds, receiving the notables at the top of a marble staircase. That's just a silly dream, I suppose."

His obvious disappointment amused her. "You never, I suppose, saw her as the wife of anything as lowly as a banker?"

"How could the wife of a banker be any kind of a partner to her husband? Would he put her behind the counter?"

"No, no, there'd be all kinds of ways!" She had not only destroyed any idea he might have nurtured that she had designs on him; she had probed him into actively promoting his own eligibility. "Look at my mother! She's invaluable to Dad. She entertains all the big depositors, organizes the firm parties, keeps the other wives happy, travels all over the world with him —"

"Stop!" She put her hands to her ears. "I take it back. Truly. A banker would do beautifully. But if you have *any* influence on my daughter, do try to persuade her not to become a vet or a dentist!"

She sent him back now to Clara, who, as she had been well aware, had all the time had her eye on them. Much later that night, when Clara came home from her date with Hoyt, she paused before her mother's open bedroom door. The latter was reading in bed.

"Did you have a pleasant evening, dear?" Violet asked.

"Mother, can I talk to you?"

"Of course, dear."

Clara came in and sat at the bottom of the bed. "You have this idea about my marrying a great man. I watched you making up to Trevor at tea. Is *he* your idea of a great man?"

"Not exactly. They're hard to come by. But he strikes me as a candidate. I think he may be a bigger banker than his father, more like his maternal grandfather."

"Oh, you've looked him up?"

"I didn't have to. I know about the family. Look, dear. These things are never sure. But it seems to me that the woman who marries Trevor Hoyt is going to have a much more interesting life than she who marries Bobbie Lester."

"Poor Bobbie. Let's leave him out of it. He's taken the whole thing badly enough as it is."

"He'll get over it. His beloved school will distract him."

"Don't gloat, Mother, or I may run back to him. Now, as to Trevor. How much does his money count in your appraisal?"

"Only as a form of insurance. If his career shouldn't pan out, then there will be lots of things that *you* can do with the money."

"Does it never occur to you that I might obtain all the things you seem to want for me — and assume that *I* want as well — on my own?"

"Oh, I've thought it over carefully. Women are going into all sorts of things now they didn't used to go into. But it's the top I'm talking about. The top jobs, except in the arts and fashion, are all tightly held by men. Maybe in the future that will change, maybe you were born a bit too early. But in a world ruled by males, a natural female leader like yourself had better pick a natural male leader."

"And that's what you think Trevor is."

"I think it's what he may be."

"So I should marry him?"

"Or someone like him."

"Marriage is the only ticket?"

"Well, it still gets you in."

"What about love? Or don't you think it counts?"

"Of course it counts. But I shouldn't think it would be so hard to love a man like Trevor Hoyt. He's obviously stuck on you, and that's half the battle."

"Yes," Clara agreed, in a more reflective tone, "there's some truth in that. It's pleasant to be loved. Unless you actually hate the person who loves you. And I certainly don't hate Trevor."

"It must be rather fun, too, to beat out all the other girls who are chasing after him."

Clara rose from the bed at this. "Do you know something, Mother?"

"I know that means you're about to say something unpleasant."

"I sometimes think you're rotten to the core." Clara's tone was as smooth as if she were uttering a compliment. "But I'm in no position to make anything of it. I'm beginning to wonder if I'm not a piece of fruit from the same tree."

"Well, as I always say, you've only one life, my girl, and the great thing is not to throw it away, as so many do. Don't ask of your nature more than it can reasonably give. That's the way the biggest mistakes are made. Will you put out the lights downstairs when you go to bed?"

"I'll put out *all* the lights!" Clara exclaimed with a rather nasty chuckle as she closed her mother's door behind her.

2

CLARA WAS TO WONDER in later years why in her middle teens she had been so concerned with her ability to fit in with the girls in her class at Saint Timothy's, that is with those of them who came from notable New York and Boston families and their boy friends whom she met on summer visits. She was at all times perfectly conscious of her own good looks and easy competence in sports and studies, and, after all, to be the daughter of a Yale college master, even to the snootiest denizen of Park Avenue or Beacon Street, was not a thing to be despised. She eventually decided that it must be the common lot of children to be forever looking up and never down Jacob's ladder, and for even the most privileged to feel bereft of every blessing in the presence of those possessed of even a minor social advantage. Yet still, in her own case, there was another factor. She wanted more things than her friends did. She wanted indeed everything that the world might not give her.

They were not all bad things, by any means. Clara had her dreams of being a Florence Nightingale, the angel of the army hospital at Scutari. She could even feel exaltation at the picture of Joan of Arc amid the licking flames at Rouen. In Mount Desert Island in Maine, where her family had a camp in the woods, she would visit her friend Polly Milton in fashionable Bar Harbor, and one day in the village, when Polly and her mother were seeing a doctor and Clara was waiting in the back of the car, a crowd of children, attracted by the tall yellow shining Hispano Suiza, crowded around it to peer in the windows. They were a fairly ragged lot — the time was the pit of the Great Depression — and they pointed fingers at Clara and jeered at her. Then the chauffeur got out of the car and shooed them away. That was all.

But it made an impression on Clara. She fully realized both the attraction and the protection of the big car. It was agreeable to be safe inside, to be able to roll away to a comfortable shingle mansion on the Shore Path and enjoy an uninterrupted view of the glittering Atlantic. But it might be equally agreeable to step out of the vehicle, to show sympathy to the ragamuffins, to win them with her graciousness, her loveliness, perhaps even to take them for a ride in the big car or buy them presents in the village. Clara conceived the joys of liberalism, a liberalism showered from a benign heaven on the poor and lowly beneath.

At school she found a focus for her energies in espousing the economic principles of the New Deal. A majority of the girls, coming from right-wing Republican families, had been oriented to an abomination of the president, whom they complacently described as a traitor to his class. But it was early apparent to Clara that those in favor of this "social revolution" included not only the great majority of the nation, but the more perceptive members of the school faculty, some of the brighter students and her own father, a grumbling but essentially loyal Democrat. It also gave her the opportunity to take a striking if unpopular position in school debates and dining hall discussions. Her high clear voice, her shaking blond head, her querying gray-blue eyes and sweeping gestures added up to a picture that her classmates were not apt to forget.

And her mother approved. "The great thing is not to be ordinary," she would say. Violet Longcope would not let herself be dragged into any prolonged discussion of the virtues or vices of New Deal legislation; she seemed to think that one should choose one's party affiliation as one would a hat or a dress to best suit one's particular appearance, and nobody knew for sure what lever she would pull down behind the green curtain of the voting booth. But Clara, who had learned, like so many daughters, to discount her father's violent masculine opinions in political matters, paid closer attention to her mother's, even when she couldn't quite make out where they would take her. She always felt that her mother had ulterior and perhaps convincing (if one only knew them) reasons for her sardonic attitudes towards matters that to others seemed life or death. And Violet, as her daughter was well aware, shared all of Clara's ambition for herself.

As the Depression lifted and the New Deal waxed into near respectability, at least among the more moderate Republicans, Clara found it needful to her image to move further left, and by the end of her freshman year at Vassar she had developed the reputation of being something of a radical. Some of the men she dated found it amusing, even provocative; others very definitely did not. And most of her girl friends felt she was going too far.

At least a temporary check was given to her leftward drift by a summer visit to the same house where she had experienced the incident of the impudent children and the Hispano Suiza: that of her friend Polly Milton. At a lunch party given by Polly's parents for a retired Supreme Court justice, venerable and idolized by the right, the conversation unhappily fell on a recent case in which our highest tribunal had startled the nation by upholding rather than invalidating a law particularly obnoxious to business interests. The vote had been five to four.

"Of course, now that the squire of the Hudson has finally succeeded in getting a majority on the Court that Congress wouldn't allow him to pack, we can expect him to bend our poor Constitution to his mighty will."

This gruff announcement from the old jurist was received by the table with respectful if silent acquiescence until Clara spoke up.

"But mightn't that also be the will of the American people?"

The judge glared down the table as if to hold his interlocutor in contempt. "Nobody's will, young lady, should affect the interpretation of our Constitution. When that ceases to be the case, our liberties and rights are in the garbage can!"

"But we're taught at college, judge, that the Constitution has often been construed to support the prevailing economic theory of the day."

"Humf! By some young red, I suppose."

"I think I even read it in a column of Walter Lippmann's."

His honor was not impressed. "No doubt you and your professors would like to tear up the Constitution altogether. Why let an old document drafted by Colonials stand in the way of any starry-eyed young radical who thinks he can legislate a new heaven? Would that suit you, Miss What's-your-name?"

"Longcope," Clara retorted coolly. "No, I think the Constitution, like the House of Lords in England, may have a useful function in acting as a temporary break to legislation that may have been too hastily passed. But necessary social measures should not be held up indefinitely by the economic creed of nine old men."

"You would prefer nine young women, I suppose."

"I think, on the whole, I would."

"Now, now," interposed a nervous Mrs. Milton, "as my revered father, the bishop, used to say when the conversation at table waxed too hot: 'We will now discuss the recent excavations in Crete!' And I might remind you, Clara, of the old saying: 'In society we pass lightly over topics.'"

After which Mrs. Milton turned all her attention to the ruffled judge to try to divert him with inquiries about his cherished garden, which bordered on her own.

Clara, for perhaps the first time in her life, felt the steely chill of unanimous disapproval. The dozen persons at the Miltons' dining room table reacted with silent shock and tightened lips to the brash young woman's impertinence to a revered and venerable figure. Even her friend Polly, cat-faced and raven-haired, of a chameleon disposition, sided with the table, and on their return to Vassar in the fall spread the word that Clara was allowing her radical theories to make a fool of herself and was no longer a reliable guest in one's parents' house. It was not that Clara was in any way ostracized, even by girls of the most unreconstructed Wall Street background, but she had lost the sparkle of a fresh and idealistic figure; she was being laughed at. There were even those who hinted that she was becoming something of a crank.

And Clara was devastated. She had as yet grown no hedge around the little rose garden of her extreme sensibility; she was still absurdly vulnerable. She chose now to see in her friend Polly all that was meretricious in the "great world" that she — solely at her mother's instigation, she now insisted — had been so assiduously cultivating. Polly was mean, snobbish, crassly materialistic and a slave to the smallest rules of fashion. And her other friends were not much better. Clara resolved that her future would not lie among such women or the type of mates she could easily predict they would choose.

It was at this point in her life that she first became aware of Bobbie Lester as a singularly attractive young man. She had known him for a year as her father's assistant and had at first associated him too closely with her family to see him in a romantic light. But that rapidly passed as she turned her eyes to new horizons, and Bobbie, as if drawn by a magnet, had immediately responded to her new attention with a passionate and flattering ardor. The impact of this had shocked her into a new vision of the future, stripped of the tinsel goals of Polly and her crowd, a life shared with this handsome and noble-spirited youth in an idealistic academy devoted to training boys in how best to serve their community. She would aid and assist him in his tasks; she would even, she already suspected, make up for his perhaps too naive and trusting nature by cultivating the senior masters and trustees of the school and smoothing his way to an ultimate headmastership!

When her mother had rudely torn the tinted glasses from her deluded eyes and she had for the first time seen poor Bobbie, not in the flesh — for that was perhaps all she *had* seen — but in the full poverty of his simple and honest self, she had known she could never marry him. She had fled, cutting her college courses, to the oasis of a sympathetic godmother in Philadelphia and had remained in seclusion for a week until Bobbie had tracked her down and followed her. At her godmother's firm insistence she had at last consented to see him, and this scene, not quite as painful to her as she had feared, ensued:

"You fell for a girl who doesn't exist, Bobbie," she told him sadly, and it came over her that she was watching herself, as she would have an actress on the stage. "When you realize that, you will be cured of your infatuation. And far better off. Believe me."

"But how can you say that? How can you say that when you're right there before me, the girl I adore?" There were actually tears in his eyes, which didn't help his cause at all. "How can you be a different Clara from the one I love? The one I'll always love?"

"There's no way that I can make this easier for you. You'll just have to learn to take it. No is no, Bobbie. Talk to my mother. She might be able to explain it to you."

"Your mother deceived me. When I went to her after you left she led me to believe that everything would be all right. Was she just playing for time?"

"I don't know. But she wasn't deceiving *me*."

And that was that.

Clara had met Trevor Hoyt at the end of his Yale senior year and of her junior at Vassar; in the fall and winter that followed he was working in his father's bank on Wall Street (he had opted, after all, to start there), and they were seeing each other every weekend, either on his visits to Poughkeepsie or hers to New York. He treated her with an easygoing, jocular, inoffensively possessive charm of manner; he talked about his being in love with her with just enough mild self-mockery not to alarm her into the idea that she was making any serious commitment. When he departed for the city or put her on a train to Vassar, he would embrace her with considerable fervor, but he did not press her for greater concessions, though she knew he had had a reputation for wildness in his sophomore year prior to an unexplained change of heart that had put him on a sounder track. As his mother had once unexpectedly put it to her: "We don't know quite what happened. Trevor suddenly grew up." That he was now a soberly directed and very ambitious young man nobody doubted. Clara at times was almost in awe of him.

It was now apparent that any social status she might have lost with Polly Milton's snotty little crowd had been wholly regained by being Trevor Hoyt's "best girl." Any lingering opprobrium for a tiresome parlor pink had vanished in the hard sunlight emitted by the House of Hoyt. Whatever it was that Clara had wanted to attain, whatever fantasy of belonging, of being in the right crowd, the *gratin*, the *société la plus fermée*, had now been achieved with a totality that made her wonder if it really existed as a state more desirable than — or even very different from — any other that she had or might have achieved. At any rate, a world once spurned was less contemptible when it smiled.

Certainly the Hoyts themselves welcomed her, almost too warmly. They evidently wanted to get their boy settled, and wasn't the lovely Miss Longcope with her bright eyes and bright mind and unimpeachable academic background just what the doctor ordered? They had no need of a dowry; money dripped from every branch of the family tree. Mr. Hoyt, as gray and gaunt and thin and silently authoritative as a great banker should be, though with a spicy reputation for marital infidelity, paid her the small, faintly smiling attention that Trevor's older sisters seemed to regard as a flattering departure from his usual reserve. They, Elena and Maribel, one wed to an aide of Mr. Hoyt and the other to a young partner in the bank's counsel, were big bony handsome women, strongly resembling their brother, with blunt but friendly manners. The Hoyt genes must have been strong, for none of the three children favored their mother, who was round and square-faced and inclined to be dumpy. Charlotte Hoyt, however, made up for her looks in the creative energy with which she dominated her family and household in all matters save those rare ones where a decisive and unappealable paternal veto was imposed.

Clara felt that Mrs. Hoyt approved of her but only after a very shrewd appraisal. She knew that Trevor's mother had listened to her talking even when she hadn't appeared to, as this remark of hers revealed:

"I enjoy so hearing you and Trevor discuss things with each other. It's not like other boys and girls at all! You really listen to each other. You actually communicate!"

But did they? Clara was beginning to wonder about that. It was not that Trevor lacked interest in herself or any keenness of observation. He would even on occasion show surprisingly detailed knowledge on subjects that she would have thought beneath or beyond his interests: obscure points of family genealogy, quaint historical incidents, famous scandals, exotic scenes from old movies. And he wanted to know all kinds of things about her own life: her courses at Vassar, her plans for the future, her politics, her interest in advertising. But there still seemed a curious lack of intimacy between them. Was it that he was like a director trying her out for a role? That he wasn't really interested in Clarabel Longcope, but only in a future Mrs. Trevor Hoyt? And that he was beginning to be satisfied that he was now in possession of all her secrets, or at least of all that he had need of?

But wasn't this what every woman suspected — if she wasn't an utter fool or unless he was — in the man who was courting her? Didn't he have every right to find out just what he was getting into? Wasn't she simply encountering an essential in the basic relationship of every man and woman? And might not an ultimate failure of intimacy be precisely the eternal difference between the sexes? Mightn't it even be love? Why else did she want to batter herself against the wall of his impenetrable armor, to press her soft body against his hard one? What else did any woman want? Why just that, of course.

On the weekend when she came home to tell her parents that she and Trevor were engaged, she embraced her mother and then whispered in her ear, so that her father wouldn't hear: "Now you can chant your *Nunc Dimittis!*"

3

THE PASSAGE of two years found Mrs. Trevor Hoyt very comfortably settled in what she liked to think of as the elegant *boîte* of a tiny duplex on Park Avenue and the weekend mistress of the tastefully redecorated red brick gatehouse of her parents-in-law's Georgian mansion on Long Island's north shore. A year-old daughter, Sandra, was well cared for by a full-time nurse, and, as a cook-housekeeper did all the rest, Clara found that she had time on her hands.

It was Polly Milton, now an assistant society editor of *Style Magazine,* who suggested that she join the staff there.

"There's a slot open working for the features editor, and I think you might find yourself the round peg."

Clara was tempted. A women's magazine had not been what she had dreamed of in her Vassar years, but no doors had been opened to her in her Hoyt world but those of charitable causes which her mother-in-law was indeed only too willing to fling wide. But these she had stubbornly resisted. They were all too much of what was expected of the wife of a rising young banker. Neither of her sisters-in-law would have considered working on *Style*. It would have been deemed "tacky" or "fancy-pants" by people who hunted with the Westbury hounds on weekends or watched polo.

"Of course, I'll have to talk to Trevor."

When she brought it up that night over a cocktail, he gave it his immediate and full attention. He asked some probing questions about the nature of the job.

"It sounds okay to me," he said at last. "And I agree that you ought to do something with that fine mental instrument of yours. Let's see what Mother says."

This was to be expected. It was not subservience; it was rank. Sometimes only her husband needed to be consulted; at others he and his mother; on rare ones Mr. Hoyt as well. Clara had so far had little trouble with the hierarchy, but she was aware that the time might come.

Marriage and the birth of little Sandra had not freed her from her earlier suspicion that she and Trevor lacked a true meeting of the minds. He had an even disposition and rarely lost his temper — never over trifles — and he showed a companionable interest in what she did with her days. He was generous with money, a dutiful host when they entertained, and his gallantry of manner with the more attractive female guests never exceeded what was expected in north shore society. But when she observed him with a group of men, as at a cocktail party when the men would cluster to discuss some political or sports event, or on a summer's night when the ladies were still secluded in the drawing room after dinner but could hear their husbands on the terrace through the open french windows, and heard his laugh, warm and resonant, rise above the others, she knew that he was at his ease in a way that he never was with her. Was she lacking in proper spousal sympathy, or was this something that was true of men in general? A simple fact that was idle to worry about?

She thought of her father and how obviously his happiest moments were at his fishing camp with other men, but then her parents' marriage didn't really count in this as it had never been a happy one. She loved her brother, and he her, yet she knew she often bored him, but he didn't count either, for everything but science bored him. She tried to discuss it with her friend Polly, who immediately asked her if something had gone wrong in the "bed department," and when reassured about this, blandly dismissed the subject with a "Men don't care about the things we care about."

Clara turned over in her mind the subject of bed. *Was* that the main point of a marriage? And if so, was hers such a success? Trevor, at any rate, had no complaints about the way she received his love, and she, despite the limitation of her erotic experience to him alone, suspected that his performance would be the envy of most of the wives of their group. He took sex very seriously indeed; he liked a variety of positions and showed a considerable past history in his dexterity, and he was always considerate and helpful in bringing her to satisfaction. And yet was it just her inexperience and romantic slushiness that made her feel, when he stripped in the bathroom and strode across their chamber, showing his fine nude figure, to join her naked in bed, that he was visiting a woman other than the lady of the downstairs drawing room, other than Mrs.

Trevor Hoyt? A woman who was his beautiful mistress? And a beloved mistress, too. Oh, yes, surely, for that night, anyway. And tomorrow night. Perhaps for any number of nights. But what of the days?

Her mother-in-law had tried to help about these. She did not overly interfere, but she was always full of suggestions if asked. She exuded the air of the born aristocrat who has never looked to anything but inherited right to support her rule. She was beneficent and good-tempered, but that, Clara felt, was because rebellion, or even the thought of it, never existed in her domain. Her two daughters, like Clara, lived near her, both in town and country, and basked obediently in the sunshine of her good will. She gave every appearance of being whole-heartedly devoted to Clara as the wife of the heir, and why not? Had she not raised her son to pick just such a girl as his consort?

The day that Clara walked over to the "big house" to consult her mother-in-law about the job on *Style* was a Saturday, and all the Hoyts were in the country. Close though the family was, there was no promiscuous dropping in; visits always had to be announced, and Clara, knowing Mrs. Hoyt's busy schedule, was not surprised to be kept waiting a good ten minutes in the big formal drawing room that looked out over a wide terrace to a lawn watered by twirling sprinklers. The high-ceilinged chamber, with its fine English eighteenth-century furniture and large family portraits, just escaped, as did the square Georgian mansion itself, being pompous, but charm and grace also eluded it. Charlotte Hoyt had built and decorated as she dressed and did her hair: appropriately for her station in life. Conventionality in nonessentials left the mind clear for bigger things. And what were they, Clara mused, as she noted, with a mild surprise, that her own portrait, recently done, had taken the place of honor over the mantel at the expense of one of her sisters-in-law?

"I am much honored," she observed, pointing to the canvas as Mrs. Hoyt bustled in.

"Well, Elena rather objected to being relegated to the dining room, but I told her we must all take our turns over the fireplace in here. Besides, you're the prettiest member of the family."

"I hope you didn't tell her that."

"Of course I told her." And of course she had. "I also told her she was going to have to watch her hip line or else watch her husband. She may not have inherited my looks, lucky child, but she's inherited some of my vulnerability to calories."

"Oh, Elena has a fine figure, Mrs. Hoyt! And she'll never have to worry about Phil. I've never seen a more devoted husband."

"But a widening *derrière* can be a tough test for devotion. Don't think *I* don't know. Which, by the way, my dear, reminds me of something I meant to speak to you about. Hamilton — your revered father-in-law — has been seeing rather too much of Mrs. Atkins lately. I don't want you or Elena or Maribel to have her for dinner or even for cocktails."

"Mrs. Atkins? Do I even know her?"

"You will. Hamilton is bound to introduce you. He has a mania for bringing his lady friends together with his family. God knows why. He's rather slowed down in that department in the last couple of years — since you and Trevor were married — so I haven't had to speak to you about it. I've always put up with his little goings-on — I'm enured to them. But when he becomes too obvious, I put my foot down. I let it be known that the family is off limits. That usually does the trick. He'll do anything for a peaceful interior."

"Mrs. Hoyt, you're wonderful! You really are."

"Nonsense, my dear. I'm simply practical. Now, as to this job on *Style,* I'm all for it."

"I'm so glad."

"It should teach you all kinds of things that women brought up as we were are not apt to learn. How the world outside society, for example, looks at society. And whether their picture of us is quite as inaccurate as we like to think. They are inclined to see us as snobbish and cliquish and overly concerned with dress and table manners and all manner of trivia. Maybe we are. Or at least more than we care to contemplate."

"Well, you're certainly not."

"But I sometimes think I go too far the other way. Maybe I'd have done better had I worked on something like *Style* as a young woman. Instead of scorning it, had I learned to analyse just what the fashionable life is made up of. Just what a dress or a hat or a table setting or a hairdo *can* be. If you really *know* something, maybe it's less apt to swell out of proportion."

Clara thought of her friend Polly's passion for detail. "If it doesn't enfold and smother you."

"Oh, don't worry. You can handle it. There may be great things in store for you, my dear."

"What things?"

"I'm not a fortune teller, but nice things, I'm sure. In the meantime you must content yourself with being our pride and joy."

Clara was not entirely easy as she walked back to the gatehouse. Had she been insidiously manipulated? It was all very well to be called someone's "pride and joy," but who was responsible for this work of art? The society that had clasped her so tightly to its bosom might also be squeezing the last drop of juice out of her. And what was that juice but the soul of Clarabel Longcope Hoyt?

4

IT WAS POLLY who suggested to Clara that she compose an article on the subject of the gatehouse, which the Hoyts had allowed her to remodel. Clara had, in her first half year at *Style*, already enjoyed a small flurry of success with a piece on the debutante ball, now swollen beyond recognition from the old-fashioned tea party to introduce one's grown daughter to the tight little world of one's closest friends and relations, to a supper dance of a thousand guests under a marquee, and another article on society's switch of summer preference from the lake to the ocean. She had developed her own wit and style, and Evelyn Byrd, the editor in chief, had taken her twice out to lunch. She was, as Polly put it, *lancée*.

"We've been a bit heavy lately on great houses and gardens," Polly now pointed out. "I think our readers would like something on how these estates can be converted to the needs of the next generation. To something smaller, of course, but smarter. Less grand but also less pompous. Your mother-in-law, so to speak, in ballet slippers."

"What a picture! But yes, I think I see it."

Polly's job had matured her. As an assistant society editor, her scope was sufficiently vague to allow her to stick a fanciful finger into other departments, and she had shown a creative imagination that her former preoccupation with the minutiae of social observances had hidden. That Clara was married while Polly was still single — and married so well — had reversed their old positions. The Miltons' Hispano Suiza was barely a memory now.

Clara went right to work on Polly's idea and motored one of the magazine's top photographers down to Long Island to take pictures of the interior of the gatehouse. He became highly enthusiastic about the project and snapped the big house and the gardens as well. It was while he was doing the latter that he was observed by the head gardener, who reported the fact to Mr. Hoyt. Clara had spoken of her article to her husband, who had manifested no objection, and she had not seen fit to seek the permission of his parents. That weekend, while Trevor was on the golf course and she was spending a morning sorting out the photographer's proofs, Mr. Hoyt walked down the drive to call on her.

"What is your project, my dear?" he asked her, picking up one of the proofs from the porch table. "Are you designing a Christmas card? This would make a fine one for Charlotte and me." He exhibited a shot of the front facade of his house.

"Well, you can have it, of course. But my project is something better than that." And here she explained to him the nature of her article.

His long gray countenance at once took on a grayer look. "You mean that these pictures would appear in a newspaper?"

"Not in a newspaper. In a magazine. In *Style*. Surely you know about *Style*. It's where I work."

"A women's periodical? No, I don't know it. I read *Fortune* and *Forbes*, but that's about it. And I'm afraid I cannot allow any pictures of this place to be published."

"Oh, Mr. Hoyt! Why not?"

"There are several reasons, but one should suffice. There is enough discontent already in the country over what radicals call economic injustices without inflaming public jealousy further with pictures of large Long Island estates. I am sorry, but I cannot allow it."

"But, Mr. Hoyt, it's a matter of my career!"

"Well, I'm afraid, my dear, that you will have to adjust your career to the exigencies of the family business. You can hardly expect to raise your daughter, Sandra, and the little brother or sister we all hope you and Trevor will soon give her on an editor's salary. Of course, if your employers have gone to any expense in this matter, I'll be glad to make them whole."

"Oh, it's not that." Clara paused, appalled at this sudden blockage of what she had been beginning to hope would be a breakthrough in her career at *Style*. She had been conceiving all kinds of sociological undertones in her piece; the reconstructed gatehouse would become the symbol of a much deeper conversion of the old principles of laissez-faire. It suddenly seemed to her that her father-in-law constituted an obstruction that had to be cleared away now or never.

"Oh, please make an exception for me, Mr. Hoyt!" she pleaded. And then she could only gasp when she heard herself add: "I'll ask Mrs. Atkins for dinner!" The laugh that she managed to utter was meant to be disarming.

It was not, and she knew at once that she had made the mistake of her life. One could *do* such things; one could never mention them. As she watched the expression of faint surprise that she had evoked on Mr. Hoyt's disciplined features fade into the blank wall that would define permanently the barrier between them — a barrier that had existed from the beginning had she only cared to look — she realized that she had been fool enough to think she could act without the only weapons, charm and subtlety, that a woman could use against Hamilton Hoyt.

"You may ask whom you wish to dinner, Clara" was his cool response. "It is hardly my function to suggest additions to your guest list."

Clara saw no need to mention her gaffe to Trevor when he came home. She was sure his father never would. He showed no great surprise on learning of the paternal veto of her project, nor did he find it of much importance. He pointed out that their friends the Clarksons in nearby Locust Valley were converting a windmill into a weekend getaway and might be glad (since he was in advertising) to be the subject of a piece in *Style*. And when Clara informed him that she was thinking anyway of quitting the magazine, he immediately exclaimed that he hoped she was clearing her calendar for a second baby! She offered neither encouragement nor confirmation of this hope.

Polly on the other hand was much distressed at the idea of losing her fellow worker. Over lunch the following Monday she protested vigorously.

"You don't have to leave over a little thing like a cancelled article! That happens all the time. Mrs. Byrd will understand."

"It's not that. I'm not so petty. It's rather that I've just been made to realize how extremely unimportant I am. Only a bit of fluff, really. A minor if decorative part of the decor of the lives of the Hoyts. I think I need some time to think it over. To find out just where I'm going."

Mrs. Byrd accepted her resignation gracefully, believing it was for family reasons, and expressed the hope that Clara would return to the job in due time, and Clara resumed the idle life of the young society matron. But she now observed the world in which she lightly moved with a journalist's eye. She had seen what it had tried to make of her. What in turn might she make of it? What would she be in another twenty-five years, as Mrs. Trevor Hoyt? She turned her scrutinizing gaze on her mother-in-law and on the latter's friends and began to make notes in a journal.

"They are apt to be large and largely outspoken, a bit on the bossy side, realistic, down-to-earth (as they conceive earth), good-humored, even hearty, more interested in each other than in men (who consist largely of husbands and sons). Many of them, indeed, seem almost to have forgotten that they *are* women, disdaining what they term feminine wiles and allures, and they wear their often splendid jewels more like adorned heathen idols than enticing females. I heard Mrs. Hoyt, confronted with the luscious rump of a Renoir nude at a benefit art show, announce laughingly to a group that included her husband: 'This is more Hamilton's department than mine!' These women are widely supposed to rule a society that is sometimes dubbed a matriarchy. But do they really? Even when the money is their own — and it very often is — they never use its power in business or politics. They hardly know a stock from a bond. All that is left to the men who are glad to hand over to them the home — and all that that name implies — in return. Mrs. Hoyt's birth and fortune were invaluable aids in her husband's rise; when he had them he had all he really needed of her."

Clara also revived her interest in the social forces that were changing the old financial hierarchies. She had always been in favor of the economic revolution that had started in 1933, and now she began to wonder if, thanks to her peculiar vantage point, she was not seeing deeper into its essentially American nature than the radical left. It was not, as she made it out, that the poor were seeking, as in communist revolts, to bring down the rich and seize their wealth. It was more that they wanted the rich to move over; they wanted to be rich themselves.

The Republican congressman from the Manhattan district where she lived, for example, was being challenged by a young liberal journalist who was the grandson of an Irish political judge who had made but then lost a fortune. Clara liked everything she read about Rory O'Connor, who, like herself, seemed to want everything in the world, from liberal rags to newspaper riches.

It was the always unexpectedly useful Polly who brought her together with this much-discussed Democratic candidate.

"Mrs. Byrd's giving a cocktail do this evening, and he's supposed to stop by for a few minutes to talk to me. It's not a party for him, but we're doing a piece on him, and it was the only time he had. He'll be late — they always are — and with few people left, when I'm through with him, you'll have your chance."

It worked out as Polly had said. By half past seven when O'Connor at last made his appearance, Mrs. Byrd's living room was almost empty, and the hostess herself had gone on to a dinner party. Clara, lingering, had plenty of time to observe the object of her curiosity as he was being interviewed in a corner by Polly.

She could see at once that his eyes were his great point; they were large, dark and deeply set — and surprisingly gentle. Surprisingly, because his short, tight, muscular torso, his high brow and square chin, his closely cropped black curly hair, seemed to betoken a masculinity that bordered on the aggressive. And indeed the silent stare with which he greeted her when Polly, concluding her own business, signaled Clara to come over, was hardly encouraging.

Taking the seat that Polly now vacated to get him a drink, Clara murmured a conventional compliment about his "vigorous and inspiring" campaign.

"Would you care to make a contribution, Mrs. Hoyt?" was his rather flat rejoinder.

"Yes, of course, but I'm afraid it will have to be a very small one. My husband holds the purse strings, and he's of a different political persuasion."

"I'm aware of that. One doesn't go into politics in this district without knowing about the Hoyts and the Bank of Commerce. We must wait until you're a widow, Mrs. Hoyt, before we can expect your largesse, and that, presumably, will not be before November."

Clara didn't mind his rudeness at all. A bland acceptance of bad manners might be the first step in getting around such a man. "Is money the only way one can help in a campaign? Can't one stamp letters or ring doorbells?"

"But those things aren't jobs for a lady like you."

"What makes you so sure that I'm a lady like me?"

"Why it sticks out all over you! Not that it's hard to look at, I'll grant you that. But I'm supposing you're one of those rich society gals who's had everything tossed in her lap without even having to ask for it. And now you're bored. You're smart enough to be bored. I'll grant you that, too. So you start peering over the back yard fence to see what sort of animals are playing out there."

"Isn't that rather brave talk for one of your own privileged background, Mr. O'Connor? I seem to remember someone pointing out to me, on a weekend in East Hampton, a big vulgar villa that had once belonged to a political judge of your name."

Ah, *that* was the note! He smiled, almost sheepishly. "So you've tracked me down! Yes, that was Grandpa. But we're still not far from the Irish bogs. He came over from County Cork, aged seventeen, with two gold pieces in his pocket and put one in the plate on his first Sunday in New York. And then went on to make a fortune — let's not inquire too closely just how. He also lost it, for he was always a gambler, but not before he had erected that palace on the dunes, which you rightly describe as vulgar, and married three of his pretty daughters to Episcopalian socialites. The Hamptons back then represented the soft underbelly of the blue bloods; the Murrays and MacDonalds got their start there, too."

"So he left you nothing? Not even the other gold piece?"

"You know it's just what he *did* leave me? He had kept

it as a good-luck token. I used to imagine it might have been what I brought my better scoops as a reporter on the *Morning Star.*"

"And what may bring you victory in November!"

"Well, that's a tough one. It's a Republican stronghold, you know. But who can tell? My opponent made an awful gaffe the other day, when he criticized the cardinal."

"You're a Catholic, of course."

"When I'm not being an atheist." Polly now appeared with his drink, and Clara rose. But he seemed to want to hold her. "Tell me, Mrs. Hoyt, would you really like to do some chores in my campaign headquarters?"

"Do you mean it? I'll be there tomorrow!"

Clara came home the next day from the O'Connor campaign headquarters on lower Madison Avenue prepared for the battle of her life. She had agreed to start work for the Democratic candidate the very next morning; she would be a part-time receptionist and part-time secretary; she had learned typing and shorthand at Vassar and was ready for any task meted out. But the Hoyts, she was beginning to learn, were not a family to be easily evaluated. She was almost disappointed at the mildness of opposition to which she now realized she had been almost looking forward.

"You know," Trevor announced, after listening to her without interruption, "it might be a great experience for you. It really might. This election is airing a lot of issues that haven't been thought out by the voters. To be in the thick of it and find out just what makes a guy like O'Connor tick could be a liberal education in itself."

"Well, I'm not planning to be a spy in the enemy's camp if that's what you mean."

"No, of course not. What an idea! Work your tail off for him. That's the game."

"Do you say that because you're so sure he'll lose?"

"I'm sure he'll lose, yes. But that's not why I say it. If I should ever get into the political arena myself, it would be a great asset to have a savvy spouse. Go to it, kid."

Which was the same note that his parents struck. They were almost proud, it seemed, to be able to point to a daughter-in-law so strikingly, so interestingly, independent. And Rory O'Connor, after all, was no wild-eyed red. He was a brilliant and able orator whose aunts were known to society. One of them was even something of a friend of Mrs. Hoyt; she had attached herself flatteringly to the wife of the great banker. And besides, he was bound to lose. He might even, like Norman Thomas, receive some right-wing protest votes from those who were weary of the long-term Republican incumbent.

If Rory himself seemed at first to have little to do with his new office worker, Clara soon discovered he still had an eye on her, for one day he brought his midday sandwich over to eat it at her desk and congratulate her on her good work.

"I didn't know you were even aware I was here," she observed.

"I wanted to be sure you were serious."

"And not just 'a girl like me'?"

"Can you blame me? We've had our share of kooky volunteers from the Social Register. How would you like to take some of my dictation?"

"For speeches? Of course, I'd love it!"

"And I'll want your comments and suggestions, too."

"You mean I'm to be a speechwriter?"

"Not quite. But you can tell your friends that."

"You mean I can tell my father-in-law?"

"You read my mind."

After that they were thoroughly congenial. Clara sometimes now took her own sandwich to his office, and they would eat together. She *did* offer him some suggestions for his speeches, but only because he had asked for them. She knew he didn't really want them. She knew perfectly what the source of his attraction was. And he was still, at thirty-three, a bachelor. What she might do about this, what she *could* do about this . . . but she had no plans and needed none. The present was just fine, tinged with a pleasant sense that she had at last started something.

He surprised her, however, by saying that he would like to meet her husband, and despite a full program, he made a point of dropping by her apartment one evening for a cocktail with Trevor. The latter was at his most attractive; they discussed different ways of financing a proposed bridge over the Narrows, going into details that left the ignorant Clara completely out.

"What a clear head your husband has," O'Connor remarked, pausing at her desk the next morning. "He's a man we'll have to deal with in the future."

"You mean he stands in your way?"

"Unless he finds it to his advantage to join us."

"That he'll never do. From where he sits, Louis Fourteenth was a Marxist."

"Don't underestimate him, Clara. That man will go far."

For some reason she felt put down. "It may interest you

to know he doesn't think you have a Chinaman's chance of winning."

"He's right there."

"Don't even think it!" She glanced nervously around to be sure no one could hear them. No one could. Rory was never caught out. "Why did you get into this fight if you thought you had no chance?"

"Because the party picked me to be the standard-bearer. They'll owe me one, so long as I don't make too bad a showing. They don't forget."

"I see. Everything has its quid pro quo."

"Everything has to. That's life."

"Maybe you'll be the one who joins Trevor. Seeing that you admire him so."

He chuckled. "I seem to have got your goat."

"Well, yes, you have. It irks me that you seem to value a conservative male a good deal more than you do a liberal female. It puts me in my place, doesn't it? As no doubt it was meant to."

"Is it overvaluing a conservative male to size him up? He's what we have to face, isn't he? He's the real thing."

"And not just a silly parlor pink like me, is that it?"

"Oh, you're not really anything quite yet, my friend. But that isn't saying you won't be. Not by a long shot. And don't worry. I'm not about to join your handsome spouse."

❦

O'Connor lost the election, to nobody's surprise, but he did better than expected, and he was by no means as despondent as the sad troop of his dispirited workers in the shabby crowded old hotel ballroom where he made his midnight concession of defeat. On his way to a private room where friends and relatives were waiting with drinks, he spotted Clara and went over to her.

"Come and imbibe with us," he invited her.

"Thanks, but I'm due home."

"To hear your husband crow?"

"Oh, he'd never do that."

"Then tell him something from me. Tell him you're coming to work for me. On the *Morning Star.*"

"Really? What'll I be? Editor in chief?"

"How about starting as a cub reporter?"

"Do you mean it?"

"Have I ever said anything I didn't mean? Even in the heat of the campaign?"

And he strode on, followed by his little crowd.

Clara knew that she should wait until the morrow before putting this new proposition to her husband, that she should wait until she had had a chance to discuss the matter coolly with her proposed new boss and find out exactly what the job entailed. But she was too excited for that; she wanted to embark upon a new life that very night, even when she found Trevor at home waiting up for her, at two in the morning and obviously the worse for the consumption of several scotches.

"Your man conceded at midnight," he observed sourly. "What have you been doing? Holding a wake?"

"Oh, Trevor, listen to me! I've got the most wonderful opportunity!"

And she told him about the *Morning Star.*

For almost the first time in their marriage he really blew up. "That *rag!* Are you out of your mind? Do you realize that's the red sheet that dragged my poor father over the coals five years ago? That accused him of tax fraud and cheating his stockholders and falsifying his balance sheets and I don't know what other God damn libels? Holy Moses, I had a bad enough time with Dad when he learned that O'Connor was connected with the *Star*, persuading him that it didn't matter because he only wrote a *column* for the damn paper and wasn't even on it at the time! But this! He'd throw me out of the damn bank if my wife worked for the *Star!*"

"But I wouldn't have anything to do with any old matter like that! I'd be on my own, Trevor, writing up my own things!"

"Clara, we're not even going to discuss it! It's out of the question! Utterly and entirely out of the question!"

"And if I decide to do it anyway?"

"You won't! You can't! Now go to bed!"

Trevor meant it about going to bed, and in the morning he left for the office after shaving, without his breakfast, in the obvious determination not to hear any more of the matter until she had had a chance to let his resolution sink in.

At ten o'clock she went to the offices of the *Morning Star* and was finally received, though only with considerable difficulty, for he was fighting off the press, by the defeated candidate. Rory looked very tired and seemed almost bored by her questions.

"Did your paper malign Mr. Hoyt?" she wanted to know.

"I don't think it did. The full story never came out. There were files that curiously disappeared. The charges against your father-in-law were dropped in the end by the U.S. Attorney, but I doubt that they would have been if the whole truth had been known."

"But he was vindicated. That's a fact?"

"In the eyes of his colleagues. And on the record."

"Doesn't that give his family some right to a grudge against your paper?"

"A grudge, no. Even if he had been innocent, it was the job of a free press to investigate the charges that were launched and the considerable evidence that then seemed to support them. If we never looked into any matters except those where the accused were found guilty beyond a doubt we might as well shut the press down now."

"I see." She nodded gravely. "Of course, that must be so. But what about Clarabel Hoyt? Where does that leave her?"

"So long as you ask me, I think it leaves her with a job on the *Morning Star.*"

"And I should tell my husband that?"

"In so many words."

"And dish my marriage?"

"I can hardly believe it would do that. And if it did, what would that marriage be worth?"

"Oh, *you* can say that."

"I can say it and do. It's like that old hymn they made even us Catholic boys sing at Andover: 'Once to every man and nation, comes the moment to decide.'"

"To every *man.*" Was his smile mocking her?

"You're making too much of it, Clara. Trevor Hoyt's too smart a guy to let you go over a newspaper job."

"Too smart? Thanks a heap!"

"All right, too loving, then. Make it as smarmy as you like."

"I don't think I want it to be a bit smarmy. Good day, Mr. O'Connor."

Her mother was in town for the day, and she had agreed to meet Clara for lunch at the Colony Club. Violet listened, silent and intent, while her daughter in bitter, clipped tones, recited the tale of the job offer and the reaction of her son-in-law. Her first comment was directed, shrewdly enough, to an inquiry as to O'Connor's advice. She nodded with a kind of grim satisfaction when she learned what it was.

"He wants to use you, my dear. What a feather in his cap to have Mrs. Trevor Hoyt on his radical sheet!"

"You think that's all it is?"

"Well not all, no. He's smart enough to know you'd be a damn good reporter. But he can lay his hands on plenty of good reporters who aren't related to the Hoyts and Trevors. And never forget he's an Irishman."

"That means he's on the make?"

"Well, let's put it that they're great ones for having their cake and eating it too. An Irishman, for example, would have no trouble marrying for money *and* for love. Both at the same time and in perfect sincerity!"

"Well, if he marries me, he won't get any money. Trevor will see to that."

"Holy God, what are you talking about?"

"I'm joking, mother."

"Well, please don't. I take it, anyway, there's no idea now of your accepting that job on his journal?"

"There *was* such an idea. Very much so. But I guess

there isn't now. And largely, no doubt, because of the things you've just said. Which were, of course, already in my mind. That Rory is using me. Or at least was planning to. I guess I have a lot more learning to do before I make any drastic changes in my life. And I think in the meanwhile I'm going right back to my old job on *Style!*"

CLARA WENT BACK to work on *Style*, and her life refitted itself into the old pattern. There were, however, two significant differences. The first was that she had told Trevor very firmly that she didn't want another baby for at least two years — the period, she insisted, that she would need to learn what sort of an editor she was or wanted to be — and he had grumblingly but not too petulantly agreed to prolong the necessary preventative measures. He obviously thought she exaggerated the importance of what to him was the idle fantasy of a women's magazine, but she gave him credit for not saying so. His mother had taught him at least the manners of a greater respect for women than that harbored by many of his friends, and, besides, he and Clara were young, and there was plenty of time for the larger family that he liked to envision. So many of his contemporaries planned for a brood of two, a boy and a girl, and maybe, if the husband prospered, a darling little "afterthought" of either sex. Trevor, as was his wont, thought in larger terms: he wanted three boys and three girls!

The second difference was by far the greater. History had begun to break into all their lives. As the war in Europe intensified and Britain seemed in danger of crumbling, Americans began to gird themselves for what now seemed an inevitable engagement in the conflict. Trevor moved across town to the USS *Prairie State*, moored in the Hudson, to become that "ninety-day wonder," an ensign in the naval reserve. At the same time his father was called to Washington to become an assistant secretary of the army, and the senior Hoyts moved to a splendid colonial mansion in Georgetown. To a skeptical Clara it seemed that the clock of social progress had been turned back and that her family-in-law, and indeed Wall Street itself, were clad in the shining armor of a militant prestige. And surely her husband in his new blue uniform was a comely John Paul Jones.

The very day after the bombing of Pearl Harbor, Trevor was placed on active duty. In only a week's time he was dispatched to the Pacific to serve on a destroyer, and Clara had to adapt herself to a single life of indefinite duration. Her mother-in-law, now high in the administration of the Red Cross, was full of suggestions about war work, including one that might involve her moving with little Sandra to the Hoyts' house in Washington, but Clara, to the consternation of her in-laws, rejected them all.

"No, I have decided to stick to my job," she announced in a tone that Mrs. Hoyt was soon to recognize as final. "People are saying this war involves everyone — civilians as well as soldiers — but that's not so in America. Not yet, anyway. This is a war for the military and the munitions factories. And I daresay they can win it. But my job is to see that my magazine survives. If we all walk out on what we're doing to make a surplus of bandages, there won't be anything for the boys to come home to."

"It's nice to think they'll still have *Style* when it's all over," Mrs. Hoyt retorted.

Clara shrugged off the crack. She was experiencing a novel exhilaration at the prospect of her new freedom with its myriad opportunities. In the year that followed she initiated a series of articles dealing with the problems of women on the home front: how to make a tasty meal under rationing without resorting to the black market; what to tell your children about why their daddy is killing other men; how to dress smartly but still in keeping with the gravity of the times; how victory might threaten women's rights and what to do about it *now;* how to hate the enemy and be a Christian. She sought contributors among famous academicians, writers, and politicians. The circulation of *Style* increased.

When Trevor came home on his first leave after a year and a half in the Pacific, they had some difficult times together. The shock of combat and the forming of friendships with fellow officers in his squadron based on the shared experience of hardship and danger, rather than on pleasures sought in the company of school and college mates of similar background, had both hardened and softened him. Trevor's life had formerly been shaped around one consistent plan. He was to rise to prominence — maybe even to fame — in the world of finance without ever losing the dash, the polish or even the hedonism of that elegant compromise between an English lord and an American cowboy: the Yankee gentleman of old New

York. Now he had questions and doubts about himself and his old life, and he was more inclined to be tolerant of others, but at the same time his belief that men could be dangerous animals that had to be dominated by strong leaders had been fortified. Clara's articles had simply disgusted him; after reading two of them he refused to look at another. She was irked.

"What are we supposed to do? We who stay home and read about battles?"

"Nothing at all! Stay home and look as beautiful as you do right now, my dear! War is nothing but blood. There's no point even talking about anything but blood. If you have to be in it, you're bloody. If you're lucky enough to be out of it, you should keep yourself as unbloody as possible."

"So I should be nothing but a doll, is that it, Trevor? A doll who waits simperingly for her man to return?"

"Ah, but if you only *knew* what that means to the man!" he exclaimed, closing his eyes as he uttered a little groan.

As a kind of therapy she wrote a piece called "How to Deal with a Spouse Turned Hero" and insisted on reading it aloud to him. He was amused at some of her humorous sallies, and it made things better between them on the last week of his leave, most of which she wisely shared with little Sandra, who was enchanted with her restored daddy with his broad smiles and broad jokes and battle ribbons. It never occurred to Trevor that Clara would publish the essay, which she did shortly after his return to the Pacific. It proved one of her most popular pieces.

Clara could hardly admit, even to herself, that she felt a

faint relief when Trevor departed; she tried to encapsulate it in her relief at being able to redevote all of her energy to her work. She was now the second editor of the magazine, directly under Mrs. Byrd, indeed at times almost substituting for her, a kind of *éminence grise.* Even the Hoyts were impressed, though there was considerable disapproval of her failure to add to her family (Trevor had evidently told them about the delay) and also a good deal of shock over the "husband-hero" article when it appeared, though Trevor's sisters defended it as a contribution to the war effort transcending an overvalued privacy. Anyway, Clarabel Hoyt's was a name that was beginning to be known.

When Rory O'Connor, now himself a near celebrity for his brilliant on-the-site reporting of the invasions of Guadalcanal and Tarawa, came through New York on his way to a new assignment in the European theatre of operations, he called Clara at her office, and she agreed at once to meet him for lunch at the St. Regis. She found him his old sardonic self, only quieter, more subdued, looking thinner and a little gray and older, yet, curiously, even more attractive. He was still very much in command of himself, but as with Trevor, and presumably with thousands of other men, the world had proved itself a tougher nut to crack than it had seemed in his old campaign days.

Clara entered at once into a discussion of his newspaper pieces, which she had read with interest. "They're vivid, of course. They're quite wonderful, really. But they show, to me anyway, a new side of Rory O'Connor. You were never so gung ho about anything before. You were like Talleyrand: *Surtout, point de zèle.* You were much more anti than pro. You were fighting for the poor, but what you really wanted was to pull down the rich. And now I seem to see the Stars and Stripes waving over your prose!"

"And you don't like that?"

"I'm sure it's reader-effective."

"But you think it's like Old Glory being rippled by a concealed fan in the ballroom of the Waldorf while our national anthem is sung?"

"Well, *you* put it that way. I didn't."

"But it's what you meant." He smiled ruefully. "Yes, we were fooled, all of us idealistic dreamers, pacifists, would-be conscientious objectors, protesters against billions for armaments. We hadn't anticipated that the next war would be a kind of crusade against Antichrist. And maybe we'll be fooled again. Maybe victory will have a nasty twist. Maybe we'll find ourselves back in the grip of a relentless plutocracy as in the Grant era after the Civil War."

"Well, if that's going to be the case, we'd better be part of it. I'd rather be on top than be trod on. It also gives us a better chance to change things, if that's what we want."

He sighed, perhaps at all she took for granted. "I envy you your detachment, Clara."

"You don't at all! You think I'm shallow and cold-hearted. But what else can I be? I'm not a soldier. And don't think I can't understand your point of view. You come home from battles where men's faces and limbs are being blown off to find me using your war to enhance my career."

"You call it *my* war. Isn't it yours?"

"Of course it isn't. Has anyone handed me a gun and

told me to invade Japan? Do you want me to be an arm-chair general, screaming for bigger battles and quicker victories?"

"No, no, you're right. War belongs to those from whom sacrifice is demanded. It may even prove a boon to the others, and you and I are the others, Clara. For don't think I'm in any way superior to you. Far from it. *I* am the one who's really enhancing my career. Making a name for myself out of other men's blood and guts!"

"Well, be proud of it, then! And remember the James family in the Civil War. William and Henry ducked the draft and became famous writers, while their two fighting brothers were badly wounded and led wretched postwar lives!"

"I haven't ducked any draft, Clara."

"Oh, I know, you were exempted. And rightly, too. But my point's the same. *We* are the lucky ones. Well, let's not knock our luck."

"You beg the question."

Clara looked at him more critically now. "You *do* think I'm terrible, don't you? You think I ought to be emptying chamber pots in some army hospital."

"You've got me entirely wrong. Indeed, I think I find your sanity distinctly refreshing. It may be a sign that the world has not gone completely mad."

"Oh, you might find there are a great many people like me. *If* they were all as frank."

Clara had to return to her office right after their lunch, but, not altogether to her surprise, he suggested that they have dinner together that same night, and she accepted, making rather falsely light of this double date by adding:

"I did have something, but I'll get out of it. We're supposed to do that, aren't we, when it's a question of entertaining the boys from overseas?" At dinner he talked to her long and seriously about what he had seen in his Pacific invasions. He was graphic, at times sombre, at times amusing, always interesting, always intense. He assumed that she wanted to listen, and he was quite right. It might have been significant that he asked only one or two perfunctory questions about Trevor and his destroyer, but when he took her home to her apartment building there was no suggestion that he expected to be asked up and certainly no untoward demonstrations in the taxicab.

But he telephoned her the next morning before she had left for the office to ask her for dinner that night, and again she accepted. It was now flatteringly evident that during his three weeks leave in the city, resettled in his old apartment, he wanted to see her — and only her — every night. His days, he told her, were spent roaming the streets and Central Park with occasional visits to museums. He had no wish to look up old friends. She sensed that she was filling a new need in him; he seemed to be clinging to her, like a spar in a troubled sea, as if her very detachment from the agony of war was a kind of reassurance that there was still a reality like the supposed reality he had left behind after Pearl Harbor. Would *that* be her substitute for military service: to have brought a temporary consolation to a despondent war correspondent? And how far should she carry it? But it was abundantly clear to a mind that was beginning to be very clear about many things that she was thoroughly intrigued by the experience.

Her mother, in town for the day on a trip from New Haven, dropped into her office to be taken to lunch.

"You're looking entirely too beautiful for the lonely wife of a sailor! What are you up to, my dear?"

"Oh, I'm sleeping with the entire Atlantic fleet. Isn't that my naval duty?"

"Lucky navy." Violet took in her daughter's freshness of complexion with an appreciative but not wholly unsuspicious glance. "I wonder if Trevor hadn't better get another leave pretty soon."

"Don't be an old bawd, Mother!" Clara checked herself. It didn't ring quite right. "Trevor has nothing to worry about. I put on my beauty in the morning for *Style* and for *Style* alone."

❖

She supposed that she and Rory would come to the point before he left for Europe. Her previsions of the experience were not stained with anxiety. Perhaps the very fact that she was not carried away by any sweep of passion enabled her to isolate the prospect of an affair from the cloying associations of her husband and child. This would be something that was hers and hers alone, a gratification of senses inert now for months, a seizure of her own rights and her own life, however temporary. The very reality of it was implicit in its being the *one* thing about her life in wartime that could *not* qualify as the subject of an article in *Style*.

And if conscience should awaken, could she not ask herself whom was she hurting? Trevor need never know. And as for Rory, he was a man who could make and live with his own decisions. Besides, did she not suspect that what he felt for her was more of an infatuation arising out of the miasma of Armageddon than any lasting love? He would settle down one day with a demure little Irish virgin who would boss his head off. They all did. And as far as the Hoyts and their family traditions were concerned, well, look at what Trevor's father so scandalously pulled off!

Rory and she after their first week had exposed to each other most of the grievances of their childhood and formative years. He had told her of his long affair with a married woman and his shorter ones with two divorcées, and how messily they all had ended, and she had been candid about the events that had led up to her marriage to Trevor. They were both ready now for something more.

The first time they copulated in his apartment — and she was very definite that that verb described what they had done better than "sleeping together" or "making love" — it had been without any previous discussion or even foreplay. He had simply opened the door of his bedroom after the second of their after-dinner drinks, and she had walked in, he following. He had even switched off the light, as if to emphasize their inarticulation and isolate the fact, and they had undressed in the semidarkness.

She had only one other man's performance to compare his with, and indeed it was very much the same. There was, however, one interesting and pleasurable difference, at least as far as she was concerned: it was she who was giving, not simply he who was taking. If she had felt with Trevor that he was perhaps too much the male, she knew that with Rory, despite all his rather brandished intellectual superiority, the female in bed with him was an equal partner. And yet she loved Rory less than she loved — or had loved — Trevor. Yes, she could feel that even in orgasm! For really, did she love any man at all? Or did she love them all? Was she a monster? Or had she simply discovered a secret of life carefully concealed from the masses? Poor things, if they didn't have love, what did they have? Love was like the heaven the church in the old days had offered to the poor to keep them from rioting.

She laughed aloud as she lay beside him afterwards.

"Was it just because I've been overseas?" he asked. "Do you feel you owe it to the boys who've been 'over there'?"

"Believe it or not, you're the first." She reached for her clothes and rose from the bed. "And I want a drink."

Dressed again, they faced each other, glasses in hand, across the coffee table in his living room.

"So I'm really only your second guy? Second in the war, anyway?"

"My second ever. I was a virgin when I married — the way you Irish men like your brides — or used to, at least. You have the honor of being my first marital infidelity."

His frown seemed to correct the lightness of her tone. "A dubious honor, I'm afraid. To have seduced an honest spouse."

"Do you really worry about that? I thought you told me you'd put all that Catholic business behind you."

"The dogma I have. But the sins have a way of sticking. And the guilt. Oh, we're great on guilt."

"Hellfire still crackles?"

"It's the last to go out."

"Well, put your mind at rest. You did *not* seduce me. If

anything, it was the other way around. I did nothing I didn't want to do. And nothing I'm not willing to do again."

"Then we can enjoy our little fling for the rest of my leave?"

"I like the way you put a limit on it. Do you think I'm the type to cling?"

He gazed at her now almost regretfully. "No, I guess you're not that. What about Trevor?"

"What about him?"

"Have you no thoughts about cheating on him?"

"Thoughts? I don't think that's quite the word for them. Let's put it that he hasn't been here for me. Not today anyway."

"You've ceased to love each other?"

"How inquisitive you are. Men can never leave well enough alone. Maybe we have in a way ceased to love each other. Maybe in a way we never really did. But that's all *now*, because he isn't here. When he comes home things may be different."

"And you'll want that?"

"I hope so."

"Then we must be very discreet."

"Isn't that always wise? Which means I should be getting home." She glanced at her watch. "Oh, definitely. But I'll just finish this drink first. Provided we don't talk about Trevor. You, dear boy, will always occupy a special place in my heart as my second man. I think the second man may play a very important part in a woman's life. He opens things up."

"You mean because he shows her what she's been missing?"

"Don't be vain! That's not what I meant at all. He opens her up to herself."

"And lets her see there may be higher peaks to climb?"

"First you're vain. Now you're vulgar. But I should be grateful, anyway, that you haven't prated about love."

"No, dear," he admitted ruefully. "I haven't prated about love."

❧

Rory was summoned to his next post in London a week ahead of schedule, and he and Clara had time for only two more sexual encounters. Thinking rather luxuriously back on them after he had gone, she enjoyed a new sense of being answerable only to herself. She even began to wonder if she had not slipped into a kind of solecism: that the world was only what Clarabel Hoyt perceived and felt, and that its morality and rules of conduct were purely of her own devising. If she was herself something of a work of art, she was also the artist. And what was sin then but a part of the backdrop against which she performed, acted, danced — yes, danced — like Salome before Herod? And the moment of ecstasy would be that when she pressed her lips against those of the severed head of the Baptist!

But the fantasies of her operatic mind came to a close as abruptly and hideously as the clap of the shields of Herod's guard that struck down the infatuated princess. Rory, covering the first-wave Normandy landings, was killed on Omaha Beach. Clara learned about it from her morning edition of the *New York Times* as she sat with Sandra at the breakfast table. There had been no cable or phone call. How could there have been?

"Mummie, what is it? You look so funny!"

"It's nothing, dear. Go and get ready for school."

Alone, she began rapidly to take in how alone she really was. Could there be an actual loss, a tragic grief, if nobody knew? Was there true sorrow without sympathy, without clasped hands, moist glances, murmured banalities? Could there be noise in a forest when a tree fell if no ear was near? But then she jumped suddenly to her feet and gasped as a wrenching spasm of pain tore at her chest. Ah, she *was* human. She did feel. It was almost a relief.

But then she was Clara again, ruefully aware that she was deprived of the dignity of a great war loss if nobody knew what she was bearing. Could she defy convention and wear mourning? But no. The last thing she wanted was to be ridiculous. She had wanted to be herself. Well, she would *be* herself. And there was no time to lose.

At the office she managed to be the usual efficient Clara, or at least to assume her appearance. Polly, of course, came in to discuss the news.

"Isn't it awful about Rory O'Connor! Have you seen him at all in the past years?"

"Oh, yes. I saw him here in town two months ago."

"Really? He was a wonderful man, I suppose."

"Oh, wonderful. This war is turning very costly. Look, dear, do you have the proofs of that day care piece?"

Somehow she got through the next few hours. But the great and totally unexpected test came when she got home. She found Trevor's sister Maribel Harper helping Sandra with a picture puzzle, or rather putting up a poor show of helping her. Maribel had obviously called with something else in mind, and she followed Clara immediately into the living room when the latter suggested a drink.

Trevor's older sister was tall and skinny with brown good looks and an air of chic which she seemed to rather wish to subdue in favor of a north shore athletic look. She was usually amiable and always intelligent, but she was culturally uneducated and intellectually lazy. She enjoyed an easy popularity in a group made up of people like herself. Clara had always found her easy to get on with, though there was a considerable mutual indifference.

"I must say, you're taking it awfully well," Maribel said suddenly as Clara handed her her drink and took a much-needed sip of her own.

"Taking what well?"

"O'Connor's tragic death."

Clara decided at once not to fence with her. "What are you implying? Rory's death is a tragedy, of course. He was on his way to becoming a great man. How else should I take it but well? You know, of course, that I worked for him in his campaign for Congress."

"I know more than that." Yet Maribel's tone was not unpleasant. It was almost matter-of-fact. "My friend Aggie Higginson lives in O'Connor's building. They share a cleaning woman. She's a frightful old gossip and told Aggie about you and O'Connor."

"So she knows I went there. So what?"

"Oh, she knows more than that. You know how they pry. She found things."

"I don't think I care to know what that woman found, Maribel."

"So you deny it? You and he weren't lovers?"

72

Clara paused to consider the situation. She didn't even mind the fact that her delay might be giving her away. She knew that she could prove her case, so to speak, in court. The wretched cleaning woman could have *seen* nothing. But did she really want to fool anybody? That was the point. *Did* she?

"I deny nothing," she said at last. "What are you going to do about it?"

"Isn't it more a question of what *you're* going to do about it?"

"What can I possibly do? Poor Rory is dead."

"Well, Mummie said —"

"Oh, so you've told your mother?"

"Didn't I have to?" Of course, any Hoyt daughter would. "But nobody else. Really, Clara, nobody else knows."

"Except all the people your friend Aggie has told."

Maribel appeared not to have considered this. "Oh, do you suppose she has?" Clara nodded resignedly. "Well, anyway, Mummie wants to know if we can put this all in the past. She telephoned me this morning when she read the news. She hopes that when Trevor comes home things will go back to the way they were before."

Trevor was in London, having been given shore duty, after three years at sea, as a naval liaison officer at General Eisenhower's headquarters. He was now a lieutenant commander; the assignment, an important one, had been procured by his father.

"Trevor and I will have to decide that when we meet again. I take it there will be no way of keeping the cleaning lady's glad tidings from his no doubt curious ears."

"Mummie thinks it's so much better that Mr. O'Connor died a hero's death. It puts a different color on things."

Clara laughed. She had not thought that she would laugh that day. "How like your mother! She's a great one at cleaning us up. Oh, yes, I see it! If I'd had a walk out with some greasy civilian, some draft dodger or war profiteer, while Trevor was fighting on the briny deep, that would be beyond redemption. Of course! But with my lover dying a hero on the beaches of Normandy while my husband is safe and sound in London and, who knows, perhaps having an affair with a lovely lady of title, that puts a different slant on things, doesn't it?"

"Clara, do you know I'm sometimes actually afraid of you? You react so differently from the way other people do."

"Well, spades are spades, my dear, no matter what we call them. And I am certainly not going to call them anything else. Whatever I've done, I'll live with!"

"Do you think Trevor *is* having an affair with a lady of title?"

"Let's hope for the title, anyway. But no, Maribel, I have no reason to suspect any such thing, except that he's a very attractive man who's been away from the sex for a long time. How's Bert doing?"

Bert Harper was a naval intelligence officer stationed in the Canal Zone. Maribel's features immediately darkened.

"You may well ask," she muttered.

6

TREVOR HOYT in London learned of his wife's affair from a letter of his mother's. Mrs. Hoyt was reserved in her statement; she confined herself to the facts and for once offered no judgment.

"Your father and I decided there was too much danger of your hearing about it from others, and it was better that you should have it straight from us. That the sorry business is over is the one good thing about the wretched O'Connor's death. Maribel is of the opinion that there's no present danger of Clara's taking up with anybody else. O'Connor, after all, was not some casual acquaintance picked up at a cocktail party; we know, of course, that he and Clara had been good friends before the war. I think, dear son, that we've all been living through very trying times, and some of us may have tumbled into strange experiences and relationships that would never have been our lot before. If you can find it in your heart to forgive this folly in your up-to-now admirable spouse, you and she may yet find happiness in the peace that seems at last to be on its way."

Trevor read the letter in his office and rose immediately to quit the building and walk briskly several times around Grosvenor Square. His seemingly cool stride belied the wrath that seethed within him. But on his third circumnavigation of the park his anger began to be qualified by an almost querulous indignation. How *could* she? How could she do this to him just *now*, when everything had been going just right in his life, when the Allied armies were pushing on to Berlin, when his own liaison work with some of the army great, including on one occasion Eisenhower himself, had been well received, when it now looked as if it might be a mere matter of months before he was back at his bank, with new friends in high places and a silver star on his chest? Oh, and then he would be more than his father's chosen successor; he would be at once his right hand and his guide!

For his time in England, amid all the brass and braid, with the scent of victory in the air and the excitement of attending military conferences at which the fabled prime minister was actually present, had done much to eclipse the Pacific years and the strain of living in a tense and tedious present with a future at the mercy of fire and water. Battle-scarred but reviving London had some of the taste and tang of his old life in Wall Street where tomorrow might always be better than today. And when Hitler's gang had been caught and hanged, had it not been in the cards that the ex–lieutenant commander and his beautiful brilliant bride would have the world at their feet?

Would have had! But now! How could she have done it? How could she have made such a hash of it? When he had had to fight a whole bloody war and had asked nothing of her but to sit comfortably on her pretty ass until it was won! Yet she had chosen to shack up with a mick reporter who had had the gall to die a fake hero before her sucker of a husband could put a bullet in his dirty gut. Well, he was dead anyway. That was something. And did she even grieve for him? According to his mother's letter, his sister had found her quite contained. Why not? She had always been a cool bitch.

His ultimate reaction was something like surprise. Surprise that he was not more surprised. There had always been something unpredictable about Clara, and he had always suspected that the unpredictable in a woman was apt to be something unpleasant. But what if she had not really cared for O'Connor? Did that make things better or worse? Better, perhaps, if he should decide to forgive and bail out his leaking marriage. Unless it meant that she was capable of casual promiscuities, which would be a distinct liability in the wife of a major bank president. But his sister had not thought that of her, and Maribel was a sharp observer, at least of that sort of thing. And certainly, if he should ever decide to try his hand at politics, an undivorced candidate might have a slight edge over a divorced one. At this time anyway. And a forgiven Clara could be kept busy making babies. One of the conditions he would surely insist on, should they reconcile, would be that they have a large family. *That* could cover a multitude of sins.

Returning to his office he found that he was able to give his full attention to a meeting to discuss the reallocation of the crew of a landing ship disabled by a flying bomb. Afterwards he felt proud of this evidence of a firm self-control. Or was he simply the counterpart of a cool bitch? And then he actually heard his own laugh. What did it matter what the world called one? It only mattered what one called oneself.

That evening he attended a large cocktail party given at the Connaught Hotel by two visiting congressmen who had crossed the Atlantic to identify their public images with a victory that now seemed imminent. Trevor found, seated at the bar, by herself for once, the celebrated figure of the comely Lady Marjorie Herron, wife of an impecunious Tory parliamentarian who was supposed to be as indifferent to her infidelities as she was to his and ever grateful for the monetary gifts that her rich admirers notoriously showered upon her. Trevor himself had had more than one fling during his English months; that was one of the differences between Atlantic and Pacific duty, and a man was a fool, in his opinion, not to take advantage of it, but Lady Marjorie, although possessed of a distinct interest in the Yankee naval liaison officer, had not featured in them. When sex was offered free, why pay for it? But now he joined her with a different attitude.

"What idiots your congressmen are," she remarked coolly. "One of those clowns asked me if I'd have had Hitler to dinner if he'd occupied London. Really, I don't think we've got anything worse in the Commons. Even on the Labor side."

"You'd have had him to dinner all right. But only to poison him."

"Just so. We'd have perished together, like that ghastly painting of Sardanapalus's last banquet. With all those nude ladies expiring by his couch. Apparently the required *grand gala du soir* in Babylon was bare ass." There was a gleam in her ladyship's eyes. Trevor recognized in her particular type of British aristocrat that rigid fusion of vanity and guts that had survived the collapse of a wall of moral duties. It was perhaps what made her such good company.

"Why are you alone here? Or are you simply fleeing the attentions of our lawmakers?"

"Well, Tommy was supposed to meet me here. But I daresay he's succumbed to the lure of some raddled royalty or wrinkled rani. Are all your American queers such snobs? Most of ours are."

Tommy, as Trevor well knew, was Colonel Thomas, a slick staff officer well known in London social circles. Lady Marjorie, for all her adventures, was something of a fag hag.

"Poor Tommy! And I thought he was such a friend of yours."

"Can a lap dog be a friend? Look, darling. You must never forget we're a nation of warriors. And we don't number among our real friends men who spent the war having tea with Emerald Cunard."

"What about me? I'm staff too."

"Ah, but you, my dear, have done your fighting. You've been carried home on your shield." She took him in now with a reappraising eye; she had already perceived that he was a different Trevor Hoyt. "Why don't we get the hell out of here?"

Trevor spent that night and several others at her flat; her husband was conveniently canvassing constituents in Wales. He did not move into the flat, for if matters between him and Clara should end in divorce, he wanted to keep his record clean. He did, however, pay Lady Marjorie's rent for a time and some other bills, which she simply handed him without comment. She herself made no secret of the fact that he was what she liked to call — adapting the phrase of Gallic kings — her *maître-en-titre* of the moment, and Trevor was the object of considerable jesting among his fellow officers. But she was nothing if not diverting, and when they parted, after his receipt of orders to report to Washington, it was even cheerfully.

"You'll be bound to be coming to London when it's all over. Bring your wife to see me; I won't bite her. We'll try to put everything back the way it was before the war. Everything except the empire. That's gone for good, I fear. If Hitler hadn't been quite so horrible, we could have divided the world with him. Now you'll see what a mess it will all be."

She almost made him think that hers had been a better world.

He could have easily arranged to go to Washington via New York and have a brief leave at home, but he wanted to talk to his mother before seeing Clara, and he didn't even write the latter of his impending return.

He met his mother on the morning after his arrival in the living room of her Georgetown house before a tray of coffee and scones. His father, of course, was at the Pentagon. It did not take them long to get down to the business at hand.

"Does Clara know that you know?"

"She must. My letters have been short and perfunctory — mostly inquiries about Sandra. And she hasn't commented in hers on my change of tone."

Mrs. Hoyt nodded. "She always knows things, that girl."

"Things?"

"Everything. Including an item about a certain British lady. But I'm not going to talk about that. I'm quite shamelessly in favor of the old double standard, particularly in wartime. I see a great difference between the understandable diversion of a fighting man and a flagrant adultery on the home front. And even in peacetime, I never regarded your father's conduct as justifying the same thing in mine. Not that I was tempted."

Trevor, gazing at those plain serious maternal features, couldn't resist a smile. "Never?"

"Well, maybe once or twice. Years ago."

"Who was he, Mother?"

"Shut your mouth. And get back to the point. I think Clara is something we ought to hang on to. *If* she'll agree to shape up in the future. You must be very firm about that."

"But even if she agrees, can I trust her?"

"Well, you know, her word would do for me. She has always been honest, at times almost too honest. And as a matter of fact, your business with the English lady may help to smooth out matters. It makes Clara look less naughty. We might even spread the word gently that she took up with her reporter in a fit of wild jealousy and revenge when she heard about you in London."

"Mother, you think of everything!"

"Like Clara? Someone has to. And there's another thing. It might be well to get her to see a psychiatrist. Not a bearded Freudian, but some doctor of our world who has common sense about these things. I miss my guess if Clara doesn't need some guidance other than from that silly crowd on *Style*."

"If she would just listen to *you*."

"No, no, family won't do. And certainly not a mother-in-law!"

When he telephoned Clara from Washington to tell her he was back and coming to New York, he suggested that they meet first in a restaurant.

"There's something I have to discuss with you before I come home," he stated flatly, "and I think you know what it is. I don't want Sandra to hear it or even to be around."

"But something you saw fit to discuss first with your mother?"

"Some aspects of which I saw fit to discuss first with Mother, yes."

"I'm sure she told you to be very stern."

"You might be surprised to learn what she told me."

"I'll make a reservation at Gatti's. It's in a brownstone on West Forty-fifth Street. Little known to our crowd."

He knew it was a mistake, but he couldn't resist it. "I suppose you've found it handy."

"Is that the spirit in which we're going to meet?"

"No. I'll be there tomorrow at one."

He was at the table on time, but he predicted that her dignity would mandate her being at least fifteen minutes late. At precisely a quarter past she appeared, and he felt a rip in his heart as he watched her long easy stride across the floor and the uncannily pleasant smile with which she managed with such apparent ease to greet him. And no, she didn't lean down to kiss him; she was just right. She seated herself comfortably and turned to him as if he were some overseas friend of an absent husband to whom she was going to be as agreeable as a good wife should.

"Well, I must say, you look wonderful, Trevor! Obviously Atlantic duty must be more salutary than Pacific."

"Shore duty is certainly healthier."

She glanced at the glass he had already emptied. "Are you going to order me a drink?"

"And a second for myself." Certainly, he needed it! What sort of an article for *Style* was this elegant creature going to write about *this* encounter? It wasn't the "hero" who was now the stranger. It was *she!*

They avoided the central topic for a few minutes as she brought him up to date on their daughter.

"You know, you mustn't be upset if she hardly knows you, or if she even resents you. Some five-year-olds do. They think you're going to take Mummie away from them — Mummie whom they've had all to themselves for so long. But I've always talked to her about you and put every snapshot you sent me on her bureau. It'll be all right. You just have to be patient for the first few days."

"I take it she likes her school?"

"Well, you know, there's not much to like or dislike about those schools. In winter it takes almost an hour to get them out of their coats and scarfs and boots and then it's time for 'juice,' which takes another hour. After that there's a third hour to get them back into their outfits and it's time to go home."

He didn't respond to this, and after a brief silence he plunged in.

"What I really want to know is whether you and I will be able to put this thing behind us."

With a firm gesture she put her glass down on the table. "This thing? Let us define it. You are referring to the fact that on three occasions I had sexual intercourse with Rory O'Connor?"

For a minute he couldn't even swallow. Could admiration turn to hate in such a flash? He breathed deeply. Yes, if the hate was already there! "It's a pity it had to be so brief, isn't it? I suppose he was ordered abroad?"

"He was. To London and then to his death."

"And you're still in mourning for him?"

"I don't think I care to answer that." All traces of her greeting smile had now vanished. "It isn't really relevant to you and me."

"Oh, but it is! What I want to find out is whether you aim to be a loving and faithful wife when I return to civilian life and try to put together the broken pieces of my old career."

"That will depend, won't it, on how you view me and what I've just told you I've done? For what I've just told you is *all* that I've done."

"And quite enough too."

"I suppose that's the answer to my question. You regard me as an abandoned and wicked woman."

"Well, those are strong words. But you know what people think of war wives who cheat on their fighting husbands."

"And that's what you think of me?"

"Let's say that that's what I *thought* of you. Your question is what I think of you now. You don't sound very repentant."

"Are you repentant about Lady Marjorie?"

"I am," he replied sturdily. "How much do you know about that?"

"You mean do I want to know how many times? Not at all. It's a question of the *premier pas*, isn't it? What I want you to tell me is why you and I are not in precisely the same boat."

"Because I only took up with Lady Marjorie after I'd learned about you and O'Connor. It was an understandable male revenge." He brushed aside the memory that this had been his mother's proposed defense for Clara, and eyed his wife closely for any prick of awareness on her part that Lady Marjorie had not been his only diversion. But her expression betrayed no such suspicion. Lady Marjorie's rank engulfed the other women.

"I can understand that," she said now, and he felt a shiver of anger that she did not resent it more. "Which is why I do not hold her against you. But I am very clear in my mind that one adultery balances another, no matter what the motive. With me, then, it was attraction. With you it was revenge. There we are. Tit for tat."

"But that's not the way the world sees it! The world that you and I will live in — *if* we decide to live in it together — will see my affair as a wartime peccadillo and yours as a betrayal. They will be able to overlook it, however, if I and my family overlook it, and you behave yourself in the future. No, you needn't look at me that way, Clara." Her lips had tightened, and her eyes were a hard blue. "You know what I mean. You can be a great asset to me if I only know you're behind me. And there's always been a side of you that hasn't been. I've known that. I've always known it. You needn't deny it."

"I *don't* deny it. That side of me has simply been Clara, a woman who doesn't want to be completely swallowed up in her husband's life."

"Swallowed up? We'd be partners, that's all!"

"Partners in *your* life."

"Well, whose else do I have? Do you want me on *Style?* Look, Clara, that other side of you, whatever it is, has been growing all during this war. Before we get back together — *if* we get back together — I want you to consult a psychiatrist. I want you to find out if you *can* be the wife I need. And if you even want to be."

"I don't need to consult any doctor. I know what I want and don't want. I'm willing to face the future with you, Trevor, but I can't give you any guarantee of what I may become, nor do I ask any about you. We must take our chances in life, like anyone else."

"That's not going to be good enough for me."

"You're not like Margaret Fuller, then. You don't accept the universe."

"Who's Margaret Fuller?"

A waiter was hovering, awaiting their order, and Clara picked up the menu.

But she knew, as she debated between the quiche and eggs Benedict, that her marriage was over. She also knew that Trevor would waste precious little time in finding a new consort more suited to his purposes in life. And he would find one easily enough. He was not a person to make a second mistake. And neither, she devoutly hoped, was she.

7

VIOLET LONGCOPE'S RECEIPT of the knowledge of her daughter's separation and impending divorce, after the Japanese surrender had seemed to offer hope for a new world, had been the final stroke in a series of misfortunes. Irving's retirement to a little cottage on the outskirts of New Haven had deprived her of most of the amenities of university life, and the heart attack that had so predictably followed his first year of enforced idleness had soured his temper and sharpened his irritability. And then her son, Brian, now teaching biology at Yale, exempted from military service because of bad eyesight, had taken up with a waitress at the Taft Hotel and was talking seriously of marriage. If she wasn't even to have Clara's brilliant life to share, however vicariously, what life remained for her?

Clara had summoned her to New York and given her the wretched news over lunch. Always that fatal midday meal! If one planned a murder it would have to be over lunch. Clara was very brief; she wished, she said, to confine herself to the bare facts, and these she laid, so to speak, on the table between their unfinished Dubonnet and their prematurely served vichyssoise.

"What madness!" Violet exclaimed.

Clara's headshake was firm. "Mother, please, it's *my* life."

"But it wasn't given you to make hash of! Well, anyway, let's look into it. Under the circumstances, what sort of settlement can you expect?"

"I don't need a settlement. I have my salary. Which, incidentally, I expect to go up."

"Until it reaches your father-in-law's? It must be some magazine, *Style*. And what about Sandra? Her clothes and nurse and school bills?"

"Oh, Trevor will take care of all that. There'll be no trouble about Sandra. She'll live with me and go to Trevor on weekends and a month in summer and major holidays. We're entirely agreed about Sandra. She mustn't be hurt."

"Except by the divorce. I see it's all very civilized. Very civilized and damnable."

"Mother, dear, you don't seem to be able to get it into your head that we're living in a different world. And, really, it shouldn't be that hard for you to face. Plenty of your contemporaries have gotten divorces."

"Yes, but that was usually because of their middle-aged husbands who lost their heads over dizzy blondes. And they were usually made to pay through the nose for their folly. But you are proposing to take nothing from a husband who, I take it, has been willing to overlook *your* indiscretion —"

"I don't consider it an indiscretion," Clara interrupted.

"Well, whatever it was." Violet paused, stultified with her sense of hopelessness. When she spoke it was almost in a wail. "When I *think* of the hand you were dealt! How could you bid anything less than a grand slam?"

"Mother, I know it's hard for you to understand. You see the Hoyts as they were in the nineteen twenties and thirties, in charge of the whole social scene: the schools, the dances, the clubs. Or even earlier, in your girlhood, at school, when Miss Charlotte Kane was the daughter of a Morgan partner, a kind of royalty, living in a pompous Beaux Arts house with twenty in help."

"Charlotte Hoyt, my dear, is not all that different today."

"No, but those people have lost their monopoly, don't you see? They still have money, but so do so many others — very different types, too. They no longer rule the roost. They don't *count* the way they did."

"But they still count."

"To you, dear. Not to me."

When Violet arrived home that evening, she found Brian visiting his father in the latter's small book-lined study. Brian was short but stocky, with short black hair, crew cut, a popular lecturer with undergraduates, now absorbed in writing a monograph on the paramecium *Woodruffi*, named for a former Yale biologist. Violet found herself wondering, as he rose to kiss her, if she had concentrated on him as she had on his sister, whether he mightn't have repaid her better than Clara had. But no, she concluded, as she drew away from him and sank wearily into a chair, he had from the beginning been too free from family ties even to resent her obvious favoritism with respect to his sibling. He had always been the scientist.

"I suppose you two are deep in the psychology of the unicellular," she remarked.

"No, Mother, we're gossiping, if you can believe it. Clara called Dad after you left this morning and told him what your lunch was going to be all about. Frankly, if she and Trevor are really set on splitting up, I'm going to try to see the good side of it."

"Oh? And what is that?"

"I think she's been kept down by the Hoyts. I think on her own she may really fly."

"Perhaps that's what I'm afraid of."

"It was you who got her into all this, Violet!" Irving's tone was shrill and raspy. "Nothing would satisfy you but to have your little girl play the great lady! You talked her out of a fine match with a fine young man. Well, I hope you're satisfied with your accomplishment!"

Violet had too long discounted her husband's moods for his opinions to matter to her. But suddenly, on top of everything else, his reproof seemed a final stone in her face. She bowed her head and started to weep.

And then Brian came over to put his arm around her with unexpected and undeserved tenderness.

"Poor Mother. Don't take it so hard. And if you're really so keen on patching things up between Clara and Trevor, why don't you go and see your old school pal, Mrs. Hoyt? Dad said that when he began accusing Trevor of ditching her, Clara interrupted him to say the divorce was really her idea. If that's the case, maybe his mother could be a peacemaker. Isn't she supposed to tell them all where to get off?"

Violet looked at him in astonishment. It was really not a bad idea.

❖

Charlotte Hoyt was in the process of reopening her stately Palladian villa on East Seventieth Street in anticipation of the early return of the Hoyts from Washington. When Violet entered the living room, whose furnishings were still covered in white cloth, she found her daughter's mother-in-law discussing plans with her caretaker.

"Bring Mrs. Longcope and me something to drink and those sandwiches I ordered, Sam," she told the dim little bald old man, "and we'll have our lunch up here."

Violet could not trace the smallest sign of resentment or hostility on the chunky features of her so matter-of-fact hostess. It was surely one of the great advantages of wealth and position — if one had the sense and wit to use them — that minor disasters could be reduced to mere inconveniences. Was a son's marriage smashed? Money would pay for a new one. A rich divorced man was quite as marriageable as a rich bachelor, and a broken heart was patchable when so many were eager to patch it. And how many hearts were broken, anyway?

"Of course, I've come to see if there isn't some way that we can get our children together again," Violet began, when the caretaker had departed. "And bring them to their senses. I don't know how much influence I have with my Clara, but I know what a strong voice you have in your own family, and I wondered —"

"Stop, Violet!" Charlotte exclaimed, holding up a hand. "Stop right now, my dear. For let me tell you candidly right now that, even if I had the influence over my chil-

91

dren that you imply, I should hesitate in this instance to use it as you suggest."

"You think that Clara's fault was so great?"

"Not at all. If that were the only hurdle, I think we could jump it. This war has taken a heavy toll on our moral senses, and a lot of things have happened that had better now be swept under the rug. No, my trouble is that I'm afraid that Trevor's and Clara's marriage has come apart at the seams. It's not only that they have ceased to be in love with each other; that might not be a hopeless objection to a reconciliation. But, much worse, they have ceased to have any goals or interests in common. Clara is all for her job now: new friends, new enthusiasms, a whole new world. And Trevor doesn't care for that world; he has a big enough one of his own. They're thoroughly incompatible. Surely you must see that."

"But with a little effort, a little compromise, on both sides?"

"That is what I originally hoped for, especially from Clara. I saw from the beginning that she had a strong will of her own, but I thought she might exercise it in a way that would push her and Trevor together as a team. But now she's got the bit in her teeth and she's going her own way. God bless her — I hope she goes far!"

"I don't see how far she'll go on a fashion editor's pay."

Charlotte blinked in surprise. "Well, I certainly give your daughter credit for not trying to hold my son up in one of those seamy alimony suits, but I hadn't thought she was reduced to what she earned on her magazine."

"What else will she get?"

"It's not what she gets, my dear; it's what she keeps.

When they were married I put a considerable sum in their joint names. Trevor tells me they've agreed to split that between them. But even half of it should make her quite comfortable."

Violet concealed her surprise. Clara had not mentioned this, and she had assumed that the whole had reverted to her husband. Half was still a hefty sum, but the whole would go far to ameliorate Clara's position in the world. Violet held her breath as her mind raced. Surely Charlotte must have known that even if the family fortune was still firmly held by the older generation and immune to a daughter-in-law's grabs, the Hoyts were getting off cheaply. A nasty lawsuit could be embarrassing to ultrarespectable bankers.

"Couldn't Trevor let her have the whole of that sum?" she asked at last.

"Why should he? It seems to me that, under all the circumstances, he's being adequately generous."

"How about this, Charlotte? Suppose they both put that money in trust for Clara's life, with income to her and the principal on her death to Sandra?"

Charlotte's immediate expressionlessness was evidence that this proposition was receiving her serious consideration. "How about on Clara's death or remarriage? I know my husband would object to any family money finding its way into the pockets of a stranger spouse."

"Fair enough."

"Well, I'll see what I can do. Though it may make something of an heiress of my granddaughter before we find her quite ready."

"Why do you say that?"

"Because the lovely Clara won't stay unmarried for long."

"Neither will your handsome and brilliant son."

Charlotte smiled, with a touch of smugness. Almost untouchable by flattery herself, she yet yielded to the pleasure of hearing any compliment to her sole male heir. "There's something in what you say there. I shouldn't be talking out of school, but you and I are such old friends that I don't mind telling you that he's already seeing a good deal of Rosie Felton."

"And who is she? Some young lovely, I suppose."

"She was Rosie Cabot. From Boston, of course. She always had a crush on Trevor, but when he married your Clara she tried to console herself with a very dear but rather dull young man called Ed Felton, who went down with his destroyer when it was sunk off the Solomons. She has a bit overdone the mourning part, but those, we know, are the first to recover. I don't think she's ever really been out of love with Trevor, and now they seem to be getting on very well. Those Back Bay blue bloods are very skillful in seeming modern when they haven't basically changed at all. Oh, for Trevor she's just perfect!"

Violet made no comment. She was sure that Charlotte was correct, and that this woman was the right match for her son: outwardly submissive, inwardly strong, and totally reconciled to every tenet of the Hoyt creed. But never mind. She had still been able to do something for Clara. She had doubled her income!

8

POLLY MILTON, three years after the war ended, found herself at the age of thirty with a good job on *Style* but still unmarried. She had a steady beau, Stuart Madison, a very serious and dedicated young diplomat, a friend ever since the old Bar Harbor days when the Madisons and Miltons had been neighbors on the Shore Path, but he was *en poste* in the Republic of Panama and not due home for a year. Stuart fully intended to stay permanently with the foreign service, which he felt was the highest of careers; it had never even crossed his mind, for example, during the war, that he had any possible obligation to offer his young and healthy body to the armed services. Neither he nor Polly had more than a pittance of inherited money, but she thought she could make up for this in the skills she had learned on *Style* in cuisine and entertainment. Such things might retain their utility, even in a postwar world.

Her own loss of any share in the Milton fortune had done much to change her life and character. Just after her graduation from Vassar her parents had undergone a bitterly litigated divorce caused by her father's infatuation with a young secretary whom he had subsequently married. Polly, who had taken without hesitation the side of a mother who had seemed palpably wronged, had renounced all further contact with him. She had done this without a thought to the financial consequences to herself, taking it for granted that any girl of her parentage and background would be looked after by the family lawyers. But when her father died, leaving the secretary as his sole residuary legatee, and her mother's improvident second spouse had lost most of her divorce settlement, Polly had had to face the chilling prospect of depending on her own talents to support herself.

In some ways it had proved a boon. She had discovered capabilities in herself, working at *Style*, that were stronger than any she had supposed. She had found the friends and acquaintances of her old idle and snobbish existence precious assets, turning their gossip and doings into material for the magazine but always in such a way as not to arouse their antagonism or alarm. She had learned to see through people; she was even beginning to see some of the stuffiness and occasional pomposity of Stuart Madison. But she also saw that he was still what she needed. She fully intended to bring matters to a head on his next leave.

And certainly nobody received a closer reappraisal from her sharpened eyes than Mrs. Longcope Hoyt, as the assistant editor in chief of *Style* was denominated after her divorce. The Polly of Vassar days would have considered her old friend a mental case to have allowed such a husband as Trevor to slip his leash, but aware now of changing values and fully appreciative of Clara's new status in the world of fashion, she had come to regard her more as a role model than a maverick. The two had remained intimate, for the care that Polly had taken not to show the smallest jealousy at having been outdistanced by her old pal had almost resulted in her feeling none.

But if Polly was dazzled by Clara's success, her mind was not wholly free from a suspicion of the calculated planning that might well be concealed in its underpinning. Was Clara, in the office phrase, a "smart cookie," or was she simply as naive as she often seemed? One day at lunch Polly explored this question further. She was telling her friend about an article she was writing on divorce settlements.

"I have to start with the biggies. The first Mrs. Marshall Field is credited with the greatest haul since Eleanor of Aquitaine divorced Louis VII of France."

"I think those things are outrageous!" Clara exclaimed. "It's notorious that the law always protects the wrong women. Like those old breach-of-promise suits. What woman worth her salt would sue a man who wants to break their engagement? She should be down on her knees in gratitude! And as for the little blondes that lie in wait for millionaires, why should they be rewarded for their cupidity?"

"Would you do away with alimony?"

"No, no, it's a matter of amounts. The husband should look after the children, of course."

Polly glanced at her questioningly. "I don't suppose you limited Trevor to that."

"I didn't take a penny from Trevor! Over what he pays for Sandra's share of my apartment and her clothes."

"Really?" Polly knew to the last penny Clara's salary

and perquisites, and she was well aware there could be no contribution from the modestly retired Longcopes. She was sure there had to be some outside funding to support her friend's life style.

"Well, I let him pay for Sandra's nurse, too, though that might be considered my expense, since it allows me to work. But he offered it, and I accepted it."

"Then all I can say is that you're a genius of a manager. *Or* a lady of considerable debts."

"I don't owe a penny, Polly!"

"How in God's name do you do it, then?"

"Well, of course, I kept what Trevor settled on me when we were married."

"Oh, you did?"

"Well, you wouldn't have expected for me to give *that* back, would you?"

"Ah no!" Polly gazed at her friend with something like awe. She could call *that* taking nothing from Trevor! Truly, Polly was in the presence of a world expert in the art of eating and keeping one's cake.

Here they were interrupted by the hand-rubbing proprietor of the restaurant who begged permission for his photographer to snap the "beauteous Mrs. Hoyt." Clara was gracious.

"Certainly. *And* the beauteous Miss Milton. Miss Polly Milton. Be sure you get her name right."

The luncheon revelation was followed by an incident that gave Polly some food for even less admiring thought. Clara had given a large cocktail party to provide the housewarming for the new apartment that *Style* had rented for her (*this* anyway had not had to be paid for by

Hoyt funds) and decorated sumptuously but cheerfully in a subdued riot of blended colors. It was to be dignified by the presence of Erastus "Eric" Tyler, the owner not only of *Style* but of the galaxy of magazines and journals of which *Style* was only a single star, though a bright one. Few of Polly's fellow workers had met Tyler, but all were acquainted with his public image: the handsome dapper graying gentleman of a youthful fifty who was reputed to hide a genius for sensing the public taste and its multitudinous variations behind a pose of aristocratic detachment.

Evelyn Byrd was, of course, to be at the party, and Clara had delegated Polly to keep an eye on the now notoriously bibulous editor in chief and keep her as far as possible from the big boss.

"And how do I do *that*, Clara? She'll be all over him like a rug the moment he comes in."

"We're using two rooms: this one and the dining room. Both should be crowded by the time he comes; he's always one of the last. I'll catch him in the hall and take him straight to the dining room, and you'll keep Evie Byrd in here. If she gets too bad, sneak her out the back and down to her car. She always has one waiting, and she's very docile after the third or fourth drink."

"But doesn't Mr. Tyler *know* about Evie?"

"He always defends her. And he's never seen her really bad. When one of the advertisers made a crack about her the other day he got quite mad. 'What do years of a blameless life do for poor Evie?' he asked me later. 'One little gin too many, and every old toper calls her a sot.'"

It turned out to be one of Evelyn Byrd's worst days. The

bonily thin, blue-haired, wrinkle-skinned lady of the sapphire eyes, tight black dress and high, high heels, so long a light of the fashion world, had evidently started her consumption even before the party, for soon after her arrival her syllables were slurred and her step unsteady. This had become a familiar enough scene to her regular companions, but that day it was a catastrophe. For Evelyn Byrd slumped to a sofa and passed out.

Polly delegated two young men from the art department to carry her down to her waiting car, but first she slipped into the dining room, where Clara was showing Tyler a Picasso bull print.

"I'm taking her through the kitchen and down the back elevator," she whispered.

"Good. I'll keep him in here."

Polly had to lead the two men carrying their inert bundle, one with his arms under Mrs. Byrd's knees and the other supporting her back, through the foyer leading to the rear of the apartment, but there, to her horror, they encountered their hostess and her peering guest of honor.

"Is that Evie?" he exclaimed. "Is she ill?"

"No, I think it may be a case of that one little gin too many," Clara retorted with a laugh she even managed to make light.

Polly could do nothing but lead her little caravan on.

Later, when all the guests had departed, and she and Clara were having a final drink while the caterer's men cleaned up around them, they discussed the shattering of their little plan.

"Tyler suddenly turned and left me to go into the hall," Clara explained. "Don't ask me why. Perhaps he spotted someone through the door who was leaving and remembered something he wanted to tell him. What could I do? You can't just grab a guest. Not a guest like that, anyway."

"You couldn't just have said, 'Oh, wait, here's another picture I want to show you'?"

"But it all happened so fast, Polly! He just went, that's all."

But Polly had a distinct picture of the couple in her mind. Clara had been *ahead* of Tyler. As if he had followed her into the hall.

"Poor Evie! He'll surely give her the sack now."

"Well, why not, Polly? What sort of a logo is it for *Style*, what sort of an image is it in the mind of an advertiser: the picture of an old girl, eyes closed and mouth open, her hat awry, being carried out of a party by two young men? The handwriting's been on the wall for Evie Byrd long enough."

And in only a week's time the prediction was fulfilled, and Clara became the new editor in chief. Polly had something to ponder in her heart.

9

LIFE FOR SANDRA HOYT, at the age of eight, had settled
into a rarely varying but not uncomfortable routine. She
took the bus in the morning uptown to the Chapin School,
where pleasant female teachers applauded her good behavior and high grades. She stayed for lunch and came
home in the bus to do her homework in the lovely bedroom that her mother had so tastefully decorated for her,
assisted discreetly by her quiet, affectionate, elderly gov-
erness, Miss Price. And when Mummie came home from
the office, always cheerful, seemingly never tired or even
preoccupied, they would have supper together — on evenings, of course, when Mummie wasn't going out to dinner — and Sandra would be told about her fascinating day
exactly as if she were a grown-up herself.

Weekends were spent with Daddy in the big new white
house that he had built on his parents' five-hundred-acre
estate in Westbury on Long Island. Daddy and his wife,
Rosie, and their little one-year-old son, Trevor Junior, constituted a new family that, together with the children of
Sandra's aunts, who also lived on the Hoyt acres, formed a

lively contrast to her solitary life in the city. There was a farm with black angus, and barns to hide in, and a maze for games and a huge swimming pool, and her cousins were nice to her — most of the time, anyway, which was all you could expect from kids. And Daddy was, as always, a sweetie pie, though he *did* prefer his golf and tennis with men friends to any romping with children. Still, that was the way with fathers; she could easily see that her two uncles-in-law were just the same.

The only troubling factor was Rosie. Not that Sandra didn't like Rosie. No, it was just the opposite. Rosie was big and brown and a fine athlete — Daddy was even willing to let her play tennis doubles with him — and she seemed so packed with good will that it seeped out of her. Sandra had at first been a bit standoffish with her, but Rosie had simply ignored this and barged her way into her stepdaughter's affections. On Friday nights, when Sandra arrived for the weekend, Rosie would sit with her when she went to bed until drowsiness overcame the tensity of her reaction to the weekly change of scene. Rosie even once did this when it involved leaving a dinner party downstairs, and Sandra learned later that her stepmother had had to pay the price of Daddy's considerable dudgeon at this desertion.

Was it being loyal to Mummie to like Rosie so much? Mummie, who was so much more beautiful and so widely admired and who did so many wonderful things for Sandra? Yet somehow everything she did was too good for just Sandra: her lovely bedroom, for example, and her party dresses, which were the envy of her school friends, the elaborate toilet set of implements with her initials in sil-

ver, the marvellous presents at Christmas and Easter —
they were really good enough only for Mummie herself.
In a funny way they *were* Mummie. Like Sandra's last
birthday party. Mummie had decided on a theme for it:
Titania's court. The living room had been strewed with
exotic trimmings; a young man from *Style* had come in to
paint a backdrop of glorious gardens, and Sandra's classmates from Chapin had been enchanted to receive ele-
gantly wrought paper crowns and wands. But there again:
Titania was not really Sandra; Titania was Mummie.

Sandra found that she wanted to know more about
Rosie; it intrigued her that her stepmother had been married to a man killed in the war. Mummie had cautioned
her not to be tactless in asking Rosie about this, but Rosie
seemed to have no inhibitions about discussing the past.
On one spring weekend, after a gardener had been summoned to retrieve the body of a woodchuck that had managed to drown itself in the pool, Sandra, walking back to
the house with Rosie, had summoned up the courage to
refer to the similar end of her first husband.

"It must be awful to be drowned," she concluded.

"They say not," Rosie answered. "Those who've been
pulled out of the water just in time. They say it's almost
pleasant, after the first gasping awfulness. I hope it was so
for my poor Ed, anyway."

"It must have been so horrible for you."

"It was, dear. But it was years ago."

"Did it make you want to die, too?"

"Oh, no. I've never wanted to die. I like living too
much."

"And then you met Daddy."

"Oh, I'd known him before. He and Ed were classmates and friends."

"Oh, yes. I remember now. Mummie told me that."

"Did she?" But there wasn't even a hint of malice in Rosie's tone. "What else did she tell you? That I had a thing about your daddy? From the very beginning? I'll bet she did."

"Did you?"

"I did. But your mother had already preempted the field."

Sandra now thought she could risk anything. "And did you still have a 'thing' about Daddy when you married Ed?"

Rosie smiled, rather wonderfully. "I'd put it away. On the top shelf of a closet in my mind that I never expected to open again. But you see, dear, life does strange things."

"Then it's all right to love two people at the same time?"

"Of course it is, dear. Why shouldn't it be?"

"I mean two people . . . well, like Mummie and you."

"Well, I should certainly hope so!"

"Suppose I told you I loved you more than Mummie? Wouldn't that be wrong?"

"It mightn't be wrong. But it wouldn't be true. You could never love anyone in the same way that you love your mother. You might at times think so. I remember having such feelings about my own mother. But take it from me, dear, those are just the natural moods of any child. And don't worry about them. Deep down, your love for your mother is a solid part of you."

Sandra gave this much thought for the rest of the

weekend, and when she arrived home on Sunday night and was having supper alone with Mummie she decided to broach a plan over which she had been brooding.

"My weeks with you and my weekends with Daddy, could they ever be changed?"

"In what way, dear?"

"Well, supposing for a year I was to spend the weeks with him in the country and the weekends with you here? Would that be possible?"

Oh, she had all her mother's attention now! And it made her tremble.

"What about school?"

"Maria — that's Aunt Elena's daughter, you know — says I could easily transfer to Greenvale."

"And is that something you want to do?"

"I think I might like to try it, yes."

"Then I'm afraid you must put it out of your mind. This is your home, my dear, and this is where you belong."

Sandra was conscious of her heart beating rapidly. Something stifled inside of her seemed about to erupt. "But suppose it was the best thing for me? Suppose the country and all my cousins and the things we do there were better for me than being in the city? Maria is always saying that!"

"Who else says that? Does Daddy say that?"

Sandra was taken aback. There was a suddenly sharp note in her mother's tone. "Oh, no."

"Does Rosie say that?"

"No, but I think she may think it."

"Well, regardless of who thinks what, my dear, you will have to reconcile yourself to going on as you've been going. You are *my* child and *my* responsibility, and you are going to have to put up with my decisions, even if they are not the ones Maria and your stepmother agree with."

"Even if they're the wrong ones?"

"Even so, I'm afraid."

"And even if I love Rosie more than I do you!" Sandra cried in a near shout.

"Even then."

Sandra stared with something like terror at her mother's unflinching gaze. "Oh, Mummie, forgive me!" she moaned, bowing her head down to the table surface.

"Why don't you go to your room, dear, and lie down until you feel calmer? I know this business of living in two places is emotionally confusing, and I think you're really coping with it well, on the whole. Miss Price is off tonight, but after a bit I'll come in and go over your homework to see that you're ready for school tomorrow."

The girl who rose and slowly trailed out of the dining room was a thoroughly defeated one.

10

ERIC TYLER had been perfectly aware of Clara's little ploy in exposing to him Evelyn Byrd's bibulous condition. It neither surprised nor shocked him. He had been too long in the publishing world not to know the ruthlessness of its competition. And women, of course, had to be even sharper than men to make up for the disadvantage of their status. Clara, whose career he had been watching with considerable interest, knew how to use her beauty and her poise as well as her fine intellect to move ahead of others, and she was also, he had noted with approval, acute enough to see just when her social position could be a liability as well as, in other cases, a distinct asset. With truculent or indurated liberals, for example, or with the kind of chip-on-the-shoulder, socially insecure reverse snobs who would find an intended putdown in any mention of a famous name, she would never allude to a Hoyt connection, a private school or a charity ball. With those, on the other hand, who liked to find in her an opening door at least to dirt about people who featured in the gossip columns, she would supply amusing and scandalous anecdotes, and even, on craftily selected occasions, a rare introduction. The more he learned about her, the more he began to see her as one of the coming "marshals" in what he liked to think of as his little Napoleonic empire.

He had never been a man to underestimate women. His own marriage, a long struggle ending in a draw, had taught him a good deal. He and the proud beautiful Lucile now lived in large separate abodes in town and country, but dined together on regular occasions and gave joint parties on holidays for their two children and the latters' friends. He well remembered, as the flotilla commander of a group of amphibious vessels in the English Channel in 1944 taking German prisoners of war to Britain, how the men had filed docilely on board, accepting defeat after years of battle and glad to be out of it, but how the women, usually nurses, had to be dragged onto the ships shrieking "Heil Hitler!" He knew which was the stronger sex.

Eric had a regular table for lunch at the Colony Restaurant, where he would be joined by the various editors of his periodicals summoned in rotation at the discretion of his all-knowing and affectionately tyrannical elderly secretary, Annie Hally. Clara was on the list, and she had added notably to the conviviality of the noon meals. One day he told Mrs. Hally that he wanted to lunch alone with her.

"Keep your eyes open," she warned him. "She's a sharpie, that girl."

"You think she'll take me, Annie?"

"For whatever you've got!"

"Not while I have *you* to guard me."

"Does that mean you want me at the lunch?"

"No! Isn't it enough that you boss me in the office?"

He was pleased that Clara did not try to make any vain point with him by being five or ten minutes late — though she had been told that they would be lunching *à deux.* She was at the table when he arrived and had already ordered herself a cocktail. For several minutes they discussed the Alger Hiss case, which was ending its second trial. Eric, as was his wont, took a balanced view.

"He may be guilty. Indeed, I rather lean to that. It's all very well to say that he was Holmes's law clerk and that Chambers is a communist meatball, but Hiss's story about how they met doesn't add up."

Clara conceded this. "But wouldn't it be better for all of us — and the country at large — if Hiss *were* innocent? If he's convicted, these crazy witch-hunts may get out of hand."

"Would you distort the facts to save him?"

"If I could do it with nobody knowing? Certainly I would!"

"Then the truth means nothing to you?"

"I'd be Pilate. What is truth? The *real* truth is that men like Hiss may have been guilty of youthful indiscretions, but they're no great risk today. All kinds of people flirted with communism in the Depression. You know *that,* Eric."

"So your 'real' truth, as you call it, is that the whole communist scare is a red herring?"

"Well, isn't it? And isn't the job of a great editor to be on the side of the real truth?"

"My trouble is that I have an old-fashioned fondness for facts."

"But you live in a world where they hardly matter. Where the issues are all!"

He regarded her glowing countenance with amusement. "And you believe that an editor, by proclaiming a truth, real or imagined, can have any significant influence on the march of events?"

"Of course I do."

"You don't believe, with Tolstoy, that we're all swept helplessly along in the turbulent river of history? That even Napoleon was like a man inside a carriage pulling at stray straps and thinking he was making it move?"

"No. I believe that Napoleon changed the history of Europe. And not for the better, either."

"But I, I gather you are telling me, should not be like him. I should be using such editorial powers as I possess for the betterment of mankind?"

"Why not? What else are you here for but to try to make things a little better? Or at least to keep them from getting much worse."

Eric was startled at the clarity of his realization that he was getting too interested in this woman. She emanated a power that was distinctly stronger than any needed to run a fashion magazine. What was it? She had a mind, certainly, but was it an interesting one? A speculative, imaginative intellect? He was not at all sure.

He decided to probe.

"Surely what you demand of me as an editor must be, at least to some degree, true of yourself?"

"Oh, yes. As you imply, it's a matter of degree."

"And was it to put yourself in a better position to improve the world, or at least to keep it from worsening, that you so neatly revealed Evelyn Byrd's little weakness to me?"

Clara was wonderful. Not the faintest blush obscured the fairness of her countenance. Her eyes widened slightly, and the hint of a nod acknowledged the justice of his observation. Her tone, when she answered, was almost matter-of-fact.

"Your discovery of Evelyn's little weakness was only a matter of time. If you had not been, as I suspect, already aware of it. If you were going to sack her, as it was inevitable that you should, you were going to need a clear episode, and I furnished you with one. It still seems to me that I handled the situation in the way that was quickest and least cruel to all concerned. And hasn't it worked out that way? The shock sent Evelyn to AA, which was where she belonged, and *Style* is now in more competent hands."

"And Eric Tyler has been successfully manipulated. Shall I continue to be?"

She smiled. "Men don't much care for manipulative women — is that what you're telling me? Well, you needn't fear me. I'm more concerned with getting behind you than getting around you. I'm happy to be on your team."

"Then I won't have to be on my guard? My secretary thinks I should be."

"The dragon? That's what we call her, you know. Of course, she thinks every woman in your organization is trying to marry you. Half of them probably are."

"But surely they must know I'm not available. It must have got around that I have an extremely retentive consort."

"Do you think that would stop anybody? It would only

add zest to the game. But Mrs. Tyler and the dragon need fear me not. I had a rich husband and I let him go. I'm not breaking my neck to find another."

It struck him, and not altogether pleasantly, that he might be letting her slam the door too hard on the possibility of other relationships. Looking at the hand with the long tapering fingers that she had rested on the table, he was seized by a sudden urge to place his own on top of it. He resisted the urge.

"I suppose word has got around the journals that my wife and I lead rather separate lives."

She met his eyes now with a frankly inquiring stare. "What am I supposed to deduce from *that* remark?"

"Simply that in the beginning of my friendship with a brilliant and beautiful woman I do not care to see our relationship doomed in perpetuity to business."

"Oh, I think we can leave the future to take care of itself," she said easily. "We're free, white and something more than twenty-one. But I'll tell you one respect in which I differ from many of my sex. I will always be perfectly frank with you. You will always know exactly what I'm up to."

"Those are brave words. From a lovely lady."

"You will find that they are true ones."

And he decided that he was going to believe her. Or at least to try to believe her.

Augustus Tyler, Eric's father, had been over forty when Eric was born in 1900, so that he belonged to a generation hatched in the Civil War and bearing lifelong, bitter traditions from the conflict that had enshrouded their infancy. As a child he had received the blessing of his grandfather's cousin, ex-president John Tyler, then a member of the Confederate legislature, and he had grown up in Richmond to become an unreconstructed Virginia gentleman who believed that the Yankee victory had turned a once proud and noble nation over to a swarm of unscrupulous and uncultivated profiteers. But where Augustus Tyler had differed from so many of his University of Virginia classmates was that he had seen that his best chance of survival was to beat the pirates of the Gilded Age at their own game. He had moved to New York and pushed his way into the railroad business and made a fortune in Union Pacific before it was taken over by Jay Gould. He never, however, changed his attitude towards either his rivals or his associates; a proud, fierce and dominating man, he refused to have social relations with any whom he regarded as of inferior class. He built himself a stone castle on Fifth Avenue and walled himself up in it like a lonely Fafner.

For his wife, a lovely Richmond belle who might have brightened life in the castle and even reconciled her husband to the more attractive elements of New York society, had died giving birth to their second child, a daughter. Augustus had been for a long period too plunged in black grief to give the proper attention to his infants — besides which he had some choked resentment of the child who had cost him her mother's life — and they were left to the care of competent servants. In time, though, he could not help but grow interested in the bright and charming boy that Eric was becoming, and this interest waxed at last into love. Yet Augustus could never quite rid himself of the uneasy feeling that this youth had been born out of time and place: that he should have been a southern planter of antebellum days and that the problems he would face in a material Yankee world were virtually insoluble. Unfortunately, he could not help sharing his gloomy forebodings with the lad. Eric invited confidences almost irresistibly.

"Old aristocracies that were rooted in the soil," he used to tell young Eric, "had some degree of stability. For better or worse they lasted for generations. But once a family is rooted in commerce it is ruled by money. The same pattern repeats itself over and over. A tycoon makes a fortune but doesn't basically know what to do with it. Or much care. The making is all. His heirs will have taste and good manners. They will buy pretty things and even contribute to pretty causes. They will dispose of Daddy's ugly mansion and erect Palladian villas. But the grand-children or great-grandchildren will let the whole thing go to pot. Some families, like the Astors, can stretch it out a bit by exercising a kind of primogeniture, but the end is always the same. You can't beat the money. It will get you, one way or another, at last."

"Then, Father, don't leave me any."

"No, no, you can't evade your destiny that easily. If I disinherited you, you'd end by hating me every time a bill came in. No, you must take your chances like everyone else, my boy. And who knows? You may be the exception that proves my rule."

Eric's youth slipped smoothly past. Possessed of charm, intelligence and the kind of glowing good looks that attract others without arousing envy, of an easy manner and gentle disposition, openhanded with the large allowance that his father freely gave him, he was popular wherever he went. At Saint Paul's School in New Hampshire he became a monitor, an editor of the paper and a near champion in the minor sports of tennis and squash; at Yale he was Phi Beta Kappa, class poet and a member of the senior society, Scroll & Key. But he had a constant feeling that it all came too easily. A harsh fellow editor of the *Yale Literary Magazine,* one who later became a famed novelist, told him that his verse was "too sweetly Tennysonian," and Eric not only agreed but incurred the man's contempt by agreeing. What was the good of his gifts in a world where business was the primary reality? And what need did he have of any gift in a business world that his father had already conquered for him?

He used to imagine that the war in Europe would either be his end or his proving ground and that he could only wait to find out which, but the armistice in 1918 while he was still a sophomore removed this solution. On graduation from Yale he was planning the postponement of any life decision by a prolonged trip around the globe when the same Yale critic of his verses, now more maturely aware of what the Tyler fortune might do for letters, suggested that Eric found an avant-garde literary magazine with them both as editors.

Eric did so, and his life changed.

The future novelist, fortunately, was brilliant, and he attracted some brilliant young writers. Eric's small but expensively printed periodical soon drew the attention of the literary world. Eric was pleased, but he always reminded himself that his success lay in promoting the talent of others. Yet wasn't that a talent in itself? Certainly, but it was a talent that needed the constant backing of wealth. Well, that he had and presumably would continue to have! The vital role of the money in his life he vowed never to understate.

His father saw the enterprise as the first step to empire; he became almost enthusiastic. "Maybe you *will* reverse the old formula, my boy! Maybe you'll become a bigger tycoon than your old man."

Augustus in his last years opened his coffers to Eric; the latter could buy anything he wanted, and he did: a stumbling fashion magazine that needed reorganization, a theatrical review, a literary quarterly, a liberal evening newspaper, a sports journal. Augustus began to take a new interest in life; he told people that the Tylers were like the Medici: he was Cosimo, Pater Patriae, and Eric was Lorenzo il Magnifico! He died almost happy. His boy had proved him wrong!

He left the bulk of his fortune to Eric after a substantial legacy to his brusque, stout, sports-loving daughter, Elmina, who had idolized him, probably because she was so obviously the less favored. Eric was now in a position to piece together a little empire of paper, and he did so, deriving both amusement and edification by adopting a variety of sometimes jibing causes. It bothered some of his editors, for example, that he should own a deeply conservative organ of the extreme right in arts and letters and a radical poetry quarterly that was constantly assailed as pornographic. But Eric's prime concern was interesting himself. He was acutely aware of just what his intellectual friends thought of him; he knew some despised him as a rich dabbler and that others suspected him of being a sinister agent of capitalist — or was it communist? — forces. Yet all treated him to constant and shameful demonstrations of flattery. He could trust none of them. But he had learned to conceal his distrust under a veneer of charm. He wondered at times if the effect of flattery was not to make one flatter oneself; was it that which made him hope that the underlying motive that justified everything he did was the quest for truth?

Because he never believed in the sincerity of his new friends and allies, because he could not assess their interest in himself as anything but their need to pick his pocket, he tended, like many of the very rich, to confine much of his social life to his economic peers. He knew that it could be a fallacy to credit these with disinterestedness — sometimes they simply craved the security and consolation of abutting moneybags — but at least they weren't always contrasting his wealth to their own poverty, and they joined him enthusiastically in the expensive sports in which he increasingly indulged: polo and court tennis. If he was as cynical as his father, at least he didn't show the rough edges. He could afford to be easygoing and agreeable so long as his life contained all the beautiful things that he desired: pictures, horses, houses and words.

It was in his quest for beauty, however, that he made his one disastrous mistake. Lucile Morris was a tall, statuesque beauty, an Astarte, with a proud manner and a small mind, the daughter of old Knickerbocker Morrises who had made their peace with new wealth. When Eric first met her, she struck him as precisely the kind of woman whom he had been destined by all the paternal predictions to marry. He was forewarned. And it was also evident from her aloofness and casual treatment of him that the propriety of his southern genealogy was obscured by the New York blinders so firmly attached to her beautiful eyes and that to her narrow social sense he was just another tycoon's son whom her father's financial plight required her to entertain. But what he had never anticipated was that such a woman could so rapidly and effortlessly enslave his senses.

For he found himself obsessed with a fierce determination to impress his image upon her. He was always cordially enough received by her parents, but she herself, even as his visits proliferated, seemed resigned, like a dutiful princess of imperial Rome, to adapt herself to the matrimonial exigencies of her family, even if they required a barbarian. Did she actually make him feel that there might be some crazy justification for his fantasy of himself as an Attila casting lustful eyes at the proud daughter of the degenerate Caesars? Or was it simply some basic instinct in her, coming down from jungle forebears, that made her do precisely what whetted his appetite the most? Certainly she was not coached in this by her mother, whose ill-disguised terror of seeing this great catch get away was almost comic.

And had he ever really thought he could make an impression on her? Or had he simply wanted to possess and crush the beautiful unresponding creature? Had his marriage been a kind of rape? Had he bound himself to an illusion? At any rate in the end he had found himself tied to a woman with whom he did not share a single important interest. His journals and his magazines, his theories and his intellectual quests, were to her only the kind of idle things a man got into if he didn't go "downtown." She was more interested in his polo, for that at least she liked to watch.

Not that they fought. They really didn't care enough about each other to fight. Lucile was entirely self-possessed; she was calm and cool in the daytime and calm and cool at night. Their two children, Tony and Lisa, were born in the first three years of their marriage; after that they did not share a bedroom. He had affairs to which she paid scant but disdainful attention; she, so far as anyone knew, had none. She seemed adequately content with the splendid separate households that they maintained in the city and on Long Island; he sometimes appeared at her parties and she at his. Her good looks became a bit hard, but she was probably as happy as her cold temperament allowed her to be. She always believed that she was right.

None of Eric's affairs had been either very deep or long lasting. Most had been with the wives of friends in Long Island north shore society; the husbands bore him little grudge as they played the same game themselves. But now, more than twenty years after his marriage, he had a foreboding that something different was in store for him. He suspected that the remarkable blond editor of *Style* was about to take over an important role in his life and that she knew it.

She was certainly nothing that his father had predicted. She had no part in the latter's arcane prophecies of what would happen to the makers and heirs of fortunes in the cycles of relentless economic history. He began to think of her as cutting the woven rope of the Norns with the silver knife of free will. But whatever she was up to, she would be amusing to watch.

11

IT WAS ONLY A YEAR after their first lunch alone that Eric relieved Clara of her editorship of *Style* and installed her in his Madison Avenue offices as the senior vice-president of Tyler Publications. She was now his right-hand man in the management of his enterprises. This had come about as the result of many further lunches and the establishment between them of a kind of partnership in the development of a philosophy that would lend some coherence to the olio of his journals and magazines. But despite the fact that they now dined together frequently and that she appeared at all his parties and he at hers, he had made no move towards a more intimate relationship. He seemed to regard their bond as something unique and presumably valuable in his life, something that might even be spoiled by any alteration. And she wondered if she didn't feel the same way.

Right after her move into the big airy office just down a corridor from his, with the splendid view across the East River to the blue and gray expanses of Queens, she had decided to tackle the formidable Annie Hally. She marched into the older lady's little room, closed the door behind her and seated herself firmly on the one extra chair.

"I'll be plain. I know you haven't wanted me here, but things will be a lot easier for both of us if we agree to work together. Let me state flatly at the outset that I have no wish to rule the roost here or to marry your boss."

"But, Mrs. Hoyt, I can't imagine who gave you the idea that I ever thought any such thing!"

"Oh, yes you can. Everyone knows everything around here. I haven't spent years in this business for nothing. But the point is that I, like you, have what's best for Eric Tyler in mind. Can we have a pact?"

Annie at this point had pulled herself together and now hugged to her chest both her dignity and her suspicions. "I don't suppose I'd last very long around here if we didn't, would I?"

"No, I'm not like that. You'll find I'm not like that at all. You have nothing to fear from me, pact or no pact. But it would be easier and simpler if we worked together."

The secretary was clearly taken aback now. It was evident that she was wondering if she could have misjudged this younger woman sitting so boldly and confidently before her. "I don't know what you mean by a pact. I should certainly like to cooperate with you in everything that concerns Mr. Tyler's best interests."

"Good. Then we're agreed. And I can explain to you now with complete candor just what my relations with Mr. Tyler are. We are good friends and business associates, and that is *all*. But if in the future that relationship should turn to one more distant — or even one *less* distant — I give you my word that I will let you know."

Annie's instant flush showed her deep embarrassment at this. "I have no wish to intrude on anyone's private life, Mrs. Hoyt."

"I'm sure of that. But nonetheless I shall keep you informed."

With Annie won over, the rest of the office had rapidly followed suit.

<hr>

Polly Milton had married her diplomat, Stuart Madison, and for the past two years had been living in Paris whither he had been transferred from Panama to be third secretary at the embassy. Clara would have thought it the perfect site for Polly, whose French was fluent, whose skills as a hostess were proficient and whose understanding of Gallic guests was acute. Yet it was not an exuberant Polly who lunched with her on a brief visit to New York for a family funeral. Her old friend seemed to have learned to view the world with a steady but unrelenting eye.

"Stuart is never going to be an ambassador," she told Clara flatly. "He's too old school, and the poor hounded State Department is anxious to show a new look. The great thing now is for a diplomat to be popular where he is sent, even if it's with horrid fascist types. We don't seem to agree with Bismarck, who said he didn't deem it a virtue in his legates to be loved in the nation to which they were accredited. *Why* were they loved, he wanted to know. What had they given away?"

"But, Polly, that should be a feather in *your* cap. You must be popular in Paris society."

"I am! But the ironic thing is that just those talents that make one popular in an old society strike the moderns as

undemocratic, snobbish and fancy-pants. The upper eche-
lons value me, all right. The ambassador calls me to act
as his hostess whenever his ailing wife is too ailing — but
that isn't what they admire or talk up. And I believe that
Stuart is actually jealous of my success. Perhaps not even
consciously. But I shouldn't be surprised if that was behind his application for a hardship post. I wouldn't be able
to outshine him giving that perfect little dinner party in a
mud hut."

"I wonder if you wouldn't. But will you really be sent
to some jungle or iceberg?"

"No, I think I've taken care of that. A little, well-placed
whimper to our ambassador. He doesn't want to lose me.
But never mind all that. Your career is what I want to hear
about. I gather you're really going places. Your fame has
crossed the Atlantic. Someone put it to me that you were
making liberalism chic."

"Of course, that someone meant it sardonically," Clara
retorted after a moment's reflection. "But I wonder if I
don't rather like it. Perhaps attractive would be a better
word than chic. We used to associate liberalism with
shorthaired mannish women and ranting, unshaven men.
And the beautiful people who did the little things well
were accused of not being able to do the big things at all.
But, damn it all, Polly, you and I *do* do the big things well!
And if I can put the left wing in black ties and ball gowns,
so to speak, maybe liberalism will actually be the better
for it!"

"Watch out they don't call you a parlor pink."

"That's the danger, of course. You've got to have charm
and a sense of humor, and you mustn't be silly. I'll send

you an interview I've just done with Senator Jack Kennedy. I miss my guess if he's not one of those surfing on the wave of the future."

"Even with that terrible father?"

"Oh, we can blot him out. Or feature him as an old dear of a survivor of a lawless age. Cuddly because his fangs have been drawn. The press can do anything, you know. And I'm pushing Eric to buy a TV station."

"Tell me about Eric. Are you and he an item?"

"No, dear, we're not."

"Then what are you?"

"You may well ask. I'm not at all sure that I know."

"Well, do you . . . ? How shall I put it, in this new day and age? As we used to say, do you fancy him?"

Clara debated this. "Oh, yes, I think so. And yet, it's funny. I'm in no hurry. I find things rather pleasant and restful just the way they are."

"And of course, he's older."

"By seventeen years. But that's not in it. Maybe that's what really suits me. Maybe it's what I've always needed in a man."

"Well, don't wait too long."

"Forgive me, my dear, but I thought you had implied that in your own case you might not have waited long enough."

"Ah, but that was in my case. Yours is a very different one. You may be on your way to proving that a great lady can still be a great man."

"Oh, Polly, what guff."

"But great as you are, you're still, I gather, dependent on this Eric. And he may be getting, at *his* age (never forget *that!*) too used to your idea of the perfect friendship. There's nothing in friendship between a man and a woman. There never has been."

"You've been too long in Gay Paree. It may be time you came home. There've been a lot of changes here."

"But perhaps not as many as you think."

"So it's your idea I must lure him to my couch?"

"Just don't stand in his way."

Clara gave her friend's advice a good deal more consideration than she admitted to her. She made no marked alteration in her behavior with Eric except to make no further references to the nature of their relationship. She had been inclined to congratulate him and herself on having worked out a uniquely satisfactory partnership between the sexes. Now she was silent about this. But she knew she was dealing with an extremely subtle and observant man. It was not long before she made out that he had flared the difference.

When he decided that the time had come to change their course, he did so in the simplest possible way. He asked her to a late lunch with him alone at their usual table on a Friday and ordered a bottle of wine, which was unusual as they typically contented themselves with a single cocktail. Just before the postprandial coffee he invited her to take the afternoon off and go with him to his apartment.

"I've given the staff the day off," he added quietly.

"Because you assumed I'd come?"

"I assumed nothing, my dear. I deduced it from a slight variation in your manner to me. Was I wrong?"

"No. I guess you rarely are."

"Then our feelings are mutual. I don't think we're going to have anything to regret."

She wondered a moment if she should ask him to define his feelings. But no, she decided, it was better this way. There was something arousing, something erogenous, in his very restraint. Suddenly she laughed.

"You know how you make me feel? Shy, almost virginal. Isn't it funny? I'm suddenly shivering like a little girl at the exciting things I'm about to be taught!"

"It may be something like that for me, too."

"You! With all your experience!"

"But what does that amount to?"

That afternoon she discovered that he was right. She knew that it was a new experience for her, and she suspected that it was one for him. Their lovemaking was gentler than what she had experienced with her husband or Rory or with either of the two men who had briefly diverted her in the more recent past, and yet it was something more intense, too. She found there was a good deal that she could do to enhance Eric's pleasure, and this filled her with a strange new tenderness, faintly filial in nature. Afterwards, when they sat silently on a sofa and listened to Saint-Saëns's organ symphony, she wondered if she could not classify her emotion, not simply as love, but as first love.

On Monday morning she went before Eric arrived to Annie Hally's office and told her what had happened. The secretary turned scarlet with embarrassment and could hardly choke out a comment, but she was overwhelmed by the compliment of so intimate a disclosure and she changed in a minute from Clara's ally to Clara's slave.

Her mother's reaction was a good deal less enthusiastic. Her father had suffered a second heart attack, which had clouded his memory and confined him to a wheelchair in the retirement home in New Haven to which they had had to move, so there was no need to take him into her confidence, but Clara knew how large a role she played in her mother's imagination and daily fantasies, and she thought it only kind to keep her up to date with her daughter's goings-on. She did so at a lunch on one of Violet's shopping days in the city.

"But, darling, an affair, that's fine, as far as it goes, but it can't go far. You can't live openly with the man."

"Why not?"

"It would be a scandal!"

"Oh, not these days. The young all do it. But I agree that I couldn't share an apartment with Eric. Not that in his world pretty much anything doesn't go, but certain appearances are still kept up. His friends, and some of mine, too, don't like things thrown in their faces. But it's perfectly acceptable for he and I to be a known thing and for us to be asked out together like a married couple."

"Isn't that already the case?"

"I guess it is. As a matter of fact, Eric and I are probably the only ones who didn't know we've been having an affair."

"But, darling child, why can't you be like other people? Why doesn't Eric get a divorce and marry you?"

"It would be terribly expensive. His wife is a very grasping woman."

"But surely he's rich enough for that!"

"Maybe, but he hates to hurt her. I think he feels guilty about having married her at all."

"Hurt *her!* What about hurting *you?*"

"Well, that's the real point, isn't it? *Me.* I'm not even sure that I'd marry Eric Tyler if he was free."

"Oh, Clara. How like you!"

"Exactly. How like me. And I intend to keep right on being like me."

Clara had further reason to feel herself a chapter unto herself, enclosed between two generations, when she tried to determine how her daughter, Sandra, felt about her frequent visits to Eric.

Sandra, now thirteen, was a dark-haired sober young lady — a lady rather than a girl — with a deeply gazing dark stare, who stood at the top of her class at the Chapin School and was possessed of a formidable memory. She treated her mother with a polite but faintly factitious affection, subject to rare but violent bursts of temper. She still went for weekends to her father on Long Island and never spoke of either parent to the other. That she judged them both, Clara was sure, and she doubted that that judgment was tempered with more than a modicum of mercy. The child was almost impenetrable.

"Is Mr. Tyler going to be my stepfather?" she asked her mother suddenly one morning at breakfast.

"Has someone suggested to you that he might be?"

"Oh, yes."

Clara didn't have to ask who. It was Monday morning, and the girl had returned the night before from the weekend visit. "Would you like him to be?"

"Well, it makes him easier to explain to people. Lots of girls in my class have stepfathers. It's a very usual thing."

"Can't you just tell people he's a friend?"

"But he's not my friend, Mummie. He's as old as some of the girls' grandfathers."

"Maybe you should call him Pops."

"I think I'm going to go on calling him Mr. Tyler."

And that was all Sandra had to say on the subject.

Clara had an easier time with Eric's daughter, Lisa, who was twenty-two, already litigating her first divorce and anxious to show her modernity by treating Clara with the same casual and faintly impudent familiarity that she had used with her father's other lady friends. Clara smoothly but firmly put their relationship on a more formal basis.

"I realize that I'm closer to your age than to your father's," she told her, "and God knows I'm not interested in being a mother figure. You've got one already, and I'm sure she's more than enough. But you must understand that, misguided though I may be, I believe I'm playing a very different role in your father's life than any of his old girl friends. Why don't you treat me as his executive officer and forget about *l'amour?*"

"Shall I call you sir?"

"It might be an excellent start!"

Lisa took this docilely enough. She needed an intermediary with her father, who was inclined to be disgusted at the mess she made of her life and financial affairs, and her mother had almost given her up. She was pretty in a rather banal blond fashion and had amiable manners, and she prided herself on her down-to-earth "what's your racket?" manner. She had convinced herself that she was superior to the older forms of snobbery and was sublimely unaware that her rebellion had been against social attitudes long superseded and that her laziness and impatience made her an easy prey to the new and subtler methods of fortune hunters and social climbers posing as egalitarians. Clara tried, with only mild success, to open her eyes to the fact that her closest pals were obvious sycophants.

Eric smiled at her efforts. He was not sanguine. "The only thing that can be done for Lisa has been done," he assured her. "I've tied up her money in an iron trust. The capital can't be invaded even for an operation to save her life. So her follies are at least restricted to her income."

Tony, Lisa's senior by two years, was a very different matter. He was a smaller and slighter version of his father with only a modest share of the latter's good looks and none of the charm. Possessed of a sharp but too literal mind, and endowed with a minimum of imagination, he distrusted his father's aristocratic disdain of public opinion and could not see any point in having publications if they did not reach the largest possible circulation. His job in the family business was to run a highly conservative but popular news magazine. Clara had no difficulty in picking up his concealed but deep distrust of her: it was only too evident that he regarded her influence on his father as just the sort that he least needed. She hardly needed Annie Hally's warning about him.

"Keep an eye on Tony. He thinks we're all fools, even his old man, and can't wait for the day when everything here will be his."

"And then what will he do with it?"

"Who knows? If we've gone communist, he'll wear a red shirt, and if we've gone fascist he'll wear a black one."

"But surely Eric knows what his only son is like."

"Tony is his father's blind spot. He's really devoted to that young man."

"And that's not an affection that Tony returns?"

"Tony's a cold fish."

Clara had many opportunities to study Eric's son. He occupied an office on the same floor and sometimes joined the paternal table at lunch. And he talked a lot. She thought she could make out, behind his highly honed sharpness and his neat punctilious appearance, a smug conviction that he could pick up whatever was essential in any public reaction to a new event or a new idea. The danger was, as Annie Hally had predicted, that he seemed to believe that whatever that reaction was, the press should go along with it. Because it *was*. And what was had to be true. Tony must have felt that there was some kind of virtue in the acceptance, by a son of privilege, of the overturning of old-caste values in a new world of equals. But didn't he also accept — mightn't so prim a fellow even favor — a future that would veer to the right (as the political trend now indeed seemed to point), that would resuscitate laissez-faire, cut taxes and welfare and even cater to bigoted religious sects? Did he not see his father's empire as too small and diversified? *He* would be a Hearst!

But how did his father see him? That had to be the point. Well, Eric certainly loved him. Of that Clara had no doubt. Tony indeed might have been the only human Eric had loved — at least until she had come along. She wondered if she could see in such paternal devotion a sense that Tony might be the proper heir of his grandfather Tyler, that he was a realist, a true man, not plagued by nagging doubts, a competent manager who could handle the people's sources of information the way the people wanted them handled and not make an intellectual parlor game of them.

Then wasn't it her job, not only for her own sake but even more basically for Eric's, to remove the bandage from his eyes? She didn't fool herself. If she were going to do it, she would have to hit and to hit hard.

It was not going to be easy, either, to find an occasion, as Tony insisted on consulting his father on business matters alone, but Annie Hally's information that he was now bad-mouthing her to the staff and her own conviction that he was trying to undermine her with his father (the sort of thing that Eric would never tell her) induced her to keep a sharp lookout. The occasion at last presented itself on a rare day at noon when the three of them found themselves alone at the luncheon table and Eric happened to ask his son about the proposed renewal of a horoscope column in Tony's news magazine.

"Can I talk to you about that later, Dad?"

"No, why not here? I'm glad to get Clara's input."

Tony glanced with muffled hostility at the proposed adviser. "It's a very popular column, as we all know."

"But we all also know it's hogwash," Clara retorted. "I think it's a disgrace to the Tyler name."

Tony's lips tightened, and his eyes roved from her to his father. "If we kill it, it may cost us a lot of subscribers."

"So what?" Clara challenged him. "What's the point of promoting trash if you don't have to? What's the point of having money if you're going to spend it lowering the already abysmally low standard of American journalism?

We might as well shut up shop and sit on a sunny beach in Florida!"

"I think it's Daddy's shop, if you don't mind my saying so. And it's up to him to shut it or not. But I hazard a guess that he believes with me that if you have a message to get across to the public, you have to have a popular organ to deliver it."

"And what, pray, is the message that you and your father are trying to get across in *your* journal? Forgive me if I haven't got it. Perhaps it was too sandwiched in between the horoscopes and your growing emphasis on violent crimes."

Tony had turned a bright pink. He faced his father. "Surely we stand for truth in reporting the news, Dad!"

But Clara was relentless. "Aren't you begging the question?"

Eric had been smiling as he watched them, for all the world, as Clara reflected in sudden irritation, as if he had been watching two cocks in a ring! Now he intervened. "I think you're being a bit hard on Tony, my dear. You have to have something you can sell if you're in the business at all."

"Of course, I realize it's a matter of degree. But catering to mass tastes can turn a paper into a rag almost before you know it. And Tony's isn't the only one in Tyler Publications that's in danger of that. Not by a long shot!"

Tony let himself go now. Perhaps he thought that her widening attack must bring his father to his side. "I suppose we must thank our lucky stars that we have the wisdom of Mrs. Hoyt between us and disaster!" At this he threw down his napkin. "I don't want any dessert, Dad. I'm going back to the office."

Eric gazed after the retreating back of his son and shook his head. "You did all that on purpose, didn't you, Clara?"

"Of course, I did. I'm tired of pussyfooting around Tony. I wanted you to see how much he hates me."

"Oh, hate, come now, Clara."

"I use the word precisely. He's determined to destroy any influence I may have in your business. I have always told you I'd be square with you. So now I'm telling you there's no way Tony and I can work together."

"You mean I'm going to have to choose between you?"

"You're certainly going to have to choose which one you listen to."

"I can't listen to both?"

"I doubt if that will work, but we'll see. What I suggest is that you deed Tony's magazine to him and detach it from Tyler Publications. That should make him happy, if anything will. Let him go his own way and see where he comes out. I'm only afraid he'll do too well."

Eric smiled, but she could see it cost him an effort. The luncheon had not been an easy time for him. "I guess the only way I'm going to achieve peace of mind is doing what Doctor Clara orders."

"And you'll find that your peace of mind is all that Doctor Clara is really working for."

12

THE NEXT TWO YEARS in the history of Tyler Publications were known as the dawn of Clara Hoyt's reign. That she was the governing force behind all the papers and periodicals was taken for granted by all but the most important editors who knew that Eric, like Louis XIV, would refuse to sign one out of ten propositions put before him to show who was still boss. And in addition, Eric, who always knew perfectly well what was going on in his business, kept a watchful eye on his partner-mistress, though he basically approved of her determined aligning of his little empire behind the liberal elements of the Democratic Party. It was certainly a change from his old policy of diversification, but that was a game he had played for years, and he was willing now to be dealt a fresh hand. There was something attractive, if still short of inspiring to him, in Clara's energy and idealism. It was fun to watch her at work, and he was getting a little old to initiate the changes himself.

Clara, of course, was conscious of his detachment and at times tried to arouse his greater enthusiasm.

"But, my dear," he remonstrated with only mild sarcasm, "you know I sympathize with your assembling of us into an army for the rights of man. But can't you see — even if you don't agree — that I might occasionally regret the old days when I had a chance to read and edit opposing opinions?"

"But, Eric, that was so passive! You were like a god on Parnassus looking down on babbling fools."

"I confess to a partiality for Justice Holmes's definition of free speech: the right of a fool to drool. But don't even liberals today still believe that truth may emerge from the clash of opinions?"

"From the clash of *intellectual* opinions, yes. But you don't get at the truth by supporting fascist or communist sheets."

"What *you* call fascist or communist. And what are you yourself, my dear, but a propagandist?"

"Everybody's that to some extent, of course. At any rate, you needn't accuse me of suppressing free speech. All those rags that you've disposed of are doing as well or better than they did under the Tyler banner. They didn't really need you."

"Did I ever suggest that *anyone* really needed me?"

"I do, anyway. Even if you think I'm a perfect ninny."

"I think *that?*"

"Well, don't you? Basically?"

"Why do you think I pay for your programs?"

"For laughs."

She always knew how to end an argument on a light note. His heart sometimes seemed to skip a beat when he realized how indispensable she was becoming to him. The freshness and light and humor that she brought to the office, always breaking off into a peal of laughter just as a discussion among the editors was verging on the sharp or even the acerb, the way she managed to meld her seriousness with her innate reasonableness, brought a pleasure into his daily work he had hardly dreamed of before. And the way she stripped herself of all the paraphernalia of her office leadership at night, the way she turned herself into a sort of geisha if he was amorous or a chatty drinking companion if he was not, made him wonder what he had done to deserve her.

Of course, he had set her up very well. She had a brownstone of her own now, lavishly decorated, and a villa in Sands Point on Long Island. He appeared at all her parties and was treated by her guests as the host. They were asked out as a couple, and he had given up attending even family dinners in the company of his wife. It seemed that everyone had accepted their liaison. Everyone but his son.

He did much thinking about his relationship with Tony. The latter had enjoyed being made sole proprietor of his magazine, whose conservative slant he had intensified and whose circulation he had increased, and Eric had advanced him additional funds pretty much as he asked, but the young man's resentment at being excluded from the management of Tyler Publications had been bitter, and, like most children, his sense of justified anger at a parent whose primary function in a son's eyes was to applaud and support him, had crippled all his efforts to flatter and appease his father. A surly Tony, with narrowed eyes and tightened lips, was not attractive, and Eric, always on the alert to view things objectively, wondered if a good part of the favor that Tony had built up in his father's heart had not been the result of a paternal desire to have a favorite child, a son and heir on whose shoulders the tired and philosophical aging emperor could lean. Might he not have been admiring the picture of his own admiration and doting?

Ah, yes, but there was something else, too. He could hardly be blind to the fact that it was Clara who had caused the rift between him and Tony, and caused it, as she had freely admitted, deliberately. Clara who, to continue his Roman metaphor, like a vestal virgin who had taken her god to bed and now, to avert the penalty of her idolatry, had to become a goddess to rule her god! It was all very well for her to insist, as she always did, that everything she undertook was in his best interest, but it was she and she alone who decided what that best interest was.

Everything, however, remained in a kind of easy balance between them until the episode of the unobtained nomination for the Senate seat. Clara had been successful in persuading him to make substantial contributions to the Democratic Party, and it had naturally followed that they were seated at fund-raising dinners and political social gatherings with the elected great. Eric enjoyed this, for the observer and editor in him was always at home in circles where power was exercised and discussed, but he received a shock when he read in a newspaper column that he was among those being considered as a candidate for the seat of a U.S. senator who had just announced his forthcoming retirement. When he asked Clara what it was all about, she replied:

"It's about what you've just asked. Or the fact that you *have* just asked. I planted the item to see how you'd react. To feel you out."

"Couldn't you have just asked me?"

"I wanted you to see it first in cold, hard print. How does it sound? The Honorable Eric Tyler. *Senator* Eric Tyler."

"It sounds unlikely. What makes you think I could pull it off? Even assuming I wanted it."

"Well, you have the looks for a senator. And much more than the brains for one. And you speak well. And you have the right friends and the right money and a press of your own."

"And you, of course. To move mountains."

"Oh, this wouldn't be my thing. I'd have to be kept rather in the background. Voters are less strict about women like me than they used to be, but there's still a lot of prejudice around. You might even have to bring Lucile forward a bit more. Don't worry; it would only be a formal reconciliation. Lucile would love to be a senator's wife and give brilliant political parties in Washington."

"Stop! How you go on! Whom have you talked to about this?"

"Only a few. But real biggies. And I'm getting some green lights."

"Without even knowing if I was interested?"

"Oh, Eric, don't take that tone, please!" Her voice pleaded now — pleaded as he had not heard her do before. "I want you to think very long and hard about this.

It's really the watershed in your career. The last real chance, as I see it, to put in some kind of memorable form all the different facets of your remarkable life and thought."

"Clara, Clara, where are you going —?"

"Oh, listen to me!" she interrupted excitedly. "You've done all sorts of things in your career, but there's always been a greatest common denominator to them: your habit of looking on."

"Say it. I'm a voyeur."

"I'd rather put it that you see yourself as a kind of silent umpire. But here's a chance to get into the real game."

"From you, dear! A cliché!"

"There you go again. The editor. The eternal editor. Puck crying, 'Lord, what fools these mortals be!' Well, I want you to be a mortal for once."

"Before mortality gets me?"

"Now who's spouting clichés?"

One of the factors that in the end persuaded him to have a run at becoming a tangible part of Clara's vision was that her project seemed no part of any ambition for herself. He had been more concerned than he cared to admit about how others might view the growing role that she played in his life. It was not altogether pleasant, despite his inward claim of being a priest of the life of reason, to suspect that he was known in his own enterprises as "Mr. Hoyt." But if Clara was actually prepared to take a kind of *Back Street* position in his life, if she was willing to dim the brightness of her own status to thrust him into the forefront of national affairs, did he not owe some sacrifice on his part in recognition of her disinterest-edness?

No sooner had he given indication to the party bosses of his willingness than he was signed up for speeches at every sort of event, from college graduations to business award dinners. The speeches he did not mind so much, as he spoke easily and knew how to evoke laughter and had plenty of help in their preparation, but he felt stifled and frustrated by the continuous handshaking and buttonholing that went on in crowded hotel lobbies, the eternal chat, the stale jokes, the scarcely veiled threats that accompanied bids for support, the factitious and noisy pose of good fellowship. And Clara, who had spoken so bravely of her own partial withdrawal from the scene, seemed more than ever in her element, brilliantly dominating groups of Democratic henchmen, smiling, nodding, giving to their wives the gingerly offered cheek to kiss that was acceptable from all well-made-up ladies. It was still, apparently, very much her business.

And then there came an incident that made him wonder if the watershed in his life, to which Clara had made reference, had not divided the river of his soul into a hundred meandering minor rivulets splashing down to nowhere. Lucile, his wife, called on him in his office, serene, poised and as sexless as a handsome marble statue. She seemed quaintly proud of herself for the oddity, or perhaps the temerity, of treading on these premises for the first time.

"Well!" she began, with a trill of laughter, perhaps not totally devoid of nervousness. "I don't know which is stranger: my being here at all or the visit I received yesterday that prompted it. For your Mrs. Hoyt called on me at home — oh, yes she did, bold as brass. If you had told me the day before that in a matter of twenty-four hours I'd not only be receiving your lady friend but actually offering her a cup of tea and then a cocktail, I'd have said you were stark staring mad!"

"There aren't many doors that Clara can't pry open."

"Pry open? She just walks in! Before I could catch my breath I found myself listening to her, entranced. For she was already in the process of convincing me that the Senate would be the best possible thing not only for you but for me and the children, in fact, for all of us!"

"Would you really like that Washington life, Lucile? It can be a worse rat race than New York."

"Well, you know, I think I would! Mrs. Hoyt persuaded me that it would be a new existence, a challenge. Perhaps just what we both need at our age, Eric!"

"So she got you on her bandwagon. And Lisa and Tony too? Clara is prodigious."

"I think she must be. And do you know something else? She may be the woman you've been waiting for all your life. The woman who can make something of you at last. God knows, I failed!"

"But you never tried, Lucile. Maybe that's why I married you."

"Bosh. You married me because you thought I was the only woman who wasn't trying to marry you. And you were wrong, as young men always are. Anyway, we can start the new regime of playing happy home by your taking me out to a very good lunch."

Eric did this, but he was not pleased at this new turn of

events in his hunt for office. It put a kind of cap on the disillusionment that accompanied his final realization that what he had regarded as the cherished jewel of his life, his independence to express his ideas and opinions, had not been simply temporarily curtailed, but removed altogether and perhaps permanently. Every speech that he gave was now carefully vetted by party hacks and often by Clara herself, and he saw that he was committing himself for the future as well as today. It was all very well for her to be lightheartedly funny about it, even witty, even sympathetically rueful, but the fact remained that his eyes, which he had liked to think of as raised to the heavens, were now fixed on the ground to avoid treading on a million sensitive toes. What permanent good could come of *that?*

"Can a politician ever say what he thinks?" he demanded when Clara handed him back the draft of a speech now covered with red pencil.

"Yes, when he takes his seat in office."

"But will he still know how to do it then? I tell you what, my dear. You go and write me another speech on tax reform, and I'll spend the afternoon writing one to express what I really believe. It will be just an exercise, but it may help me for once to write something I like."

"As long as you don't become intoxicated with the sound of your own words. And deliver it!"

"That would be the day, wouldn't it?"

He enjoyed himself thoroughly that afternoon, expounding all of his favorite tax theories. He was Daniel Webster, at least to his Dictaphone. All meals at restaurants and drinks at bars, all tickets to theatres and sports events, all outings to country clubs and conferences held in Pacific or Caribbean paradises, would become the sole responsibility of the corporate or individual host with no allowable deduction on the income tax return. This would not hurt the spender, he argued, because equal treatment would be meted out to his competitors. All would be in the same boat, and all would soon give up these bribes to customers and clients. Why, he demanded, should sober citizens in the Bible belt be required to shoulder the burden of taxes increased by the huge deductions claimed for urban entertainments that they could not afford and of which they probably strongly disapproved? And necessary business travel should be limited to tourist rates, and charitable deductions confined to sums donated to strictly American causes. And contributions to religious organizations, he finally insisted, should be carefully scrutinized to ensure that the money was not being syphoned off into social clubs and fishing camps. He ended by citing a case where an entertainment deduction had been found on audit to include the expenses of taking a group of businessmen to a brothel!

Clara came in when he had finished with the revised draft of the tax reform speech he was to deliver that night at a dinner benefitting Legal Aid. She was not to attend the dinner, as she had an annual party (fully deductible, he observed) for the editors and staff of *Style,* but she would drop in later. He let her listen to his afternoon's dictated work. Her face was expressionless as she did so.

"Well, that would have done it, of course," she said when she had finished.

"Done what?"

"Eclipsed any chance you still had of obtaining the nomination. Oh, perfectly! It's tailor-made for that. Every man or woman having the smallest interest in a restaurant or theatre or hotel — or even a cat house — would be against you. The railroads, the airlines, the tax and limo drivers, the charterers of yachts and sailboats, would all want your head. And if that's not enough you'd have alienated all the religious nuts as well. It's a clean sweep! Even the foundations!"

"It does rather clear the air, doesn't it?"

She shook her head, but then, after a moment's reflection, she seemed to be trying a more sympathetic tone. "Poor dear man, it's what you'd really like to do, isn't it? Spit in the eye of the world and tell it to go hang."

"Oh, it's just a mood."

"Is it? Are you sure? Maybe I'd better skip my dinner and go with you to the Waldorf tonight. To keep an eye on you."

"Oh, I'll be good."

But when he dressed that night for his party he slipped the copy of the Dictaphone speech which Annie Hally had rapidly typed for him into a side pocket of his dinner jacket while placing the Clara draft in the one by his chest, where it would be most available when he rose to go to the dais.

When the time came for him to speak, and he was casting a prefatory eye over the filled tables, he noted Lucile in a shimmering white gown with diamonds, too many diamonds, seated directly below him. She nodded at him with a broad and somehow proprietary smile, as though his glance had been a personal greeting; her attitude seemed to proclaim that he had been given back to her and that the deed of gift contained a clause abrogating a lifetime of precarious, perhaps even querulous, independence. Eric Tyler had been returned to nothing from nothing.

The hand that reached not into the vest pocket but the side one and withdrew the oration of his fantasy seemed guided by an impulse not his own. He closed his eyes for a moment and then reached for the glass of water to take a sip; he could sense in his audience the immediate concern that he might be ill. He corrected this with a smile and then, recklessly, nervously, delivered his speech.

The applause, when he had finished, was perfunctory. People, he reflected as he resumed his seat, will always applaud. It is an instinct of good manners. But those at his table offered no comment, and when, a few minutes later, the room rose to leave, he encountered Clara waiting at one of the doors. She had come in late from her own party, but he could tell from her fixed countenance that she had heard his talk. Or at least enough of it. She followed him without a word to his limousine.

"Shouldn't I be taking Lucile home?" he asked her.

"That won't matter now," she retorted, getting into the back of the car. "You can drop me at my place."

It was raining as they drove up Park Avenue, and Clara spoke no word. The glass partition behind the chauffeur might have separated them as well; he wondered if he spoke if she would even hear. And then a strange and irrelevant memory intruded itself sharply on his mind. He was at home, his boyhood home, in the gray stone castle on Fifth Avenue, long torn down, on the day of his first

Christmas vacation from Saint Paul's School, and he was telling Bridie, his old Irish nurse, no longer needed as such but charitably kept on by his father as an extra chambermaid, of all his adventures in his new life away from New York. And he was aware, painfully aware, despite all her enthusiastic smiles and nods, of her utter inability to take in any of the strange details of life in a boys' academy that she had never seen, much less understood. And he realized, with a rip in his heart, that what she *did* take in, with the humble resignation of a peasant woman in the chorus of a Greek tragedy, was that the gods, as had always been foretold, had taken her little boy away from her forever.

Now what, he asked himself, in the name of blazes did poor old Bridie have to do with the brilliant Clara? Was it simply that they both conveyed the message that he had done something to his life that could never be undone?

He spoke at last. "You think I did it on purpose to blow my chances for the nomination."

She did not avert her gaze from the rain on the window. "I'm not sure *why* you did it. All I know is what you succeeded in doing. They won't run you for dogcatcher now."

"You can't understand that I wanted to find out if a man can be in politics and still have principles?"

"Oh, don't give me that!" she exclaimed in sudden impatience. "You crafted that speech to outrage every voters' bloc in the city! That's not high-mindedness or even independence. It's suicide, plain and simple. If you can make something noble out of suicide, do so!"

"But if it was suicide it was only the suicide of the incipient politician. I hope you think there's a man left. Perhaps even a man of some guts." As she said nothing he continued in a voice that betrayed something like alarm: "Or is that not so? Was it only the politician-to-be that you cared about? *If* you cared at all."

"The man I thought I cared about would not have destroyed everything I've worked for to satisfy a whim." She turned to him now with anger in her eyes but then as suddenly relented. "Oh, I suppose it was a mistake to attach myself so strongly to the destinies of another. We all have our own lives to lead and only our own. You've listened to me, I admit. You may have even appreciated for a while what I was trying to do for you. But when it came right down to the point, you couldn't go through with it. Basically, you just wanted to be let alone. And why not?"

"I don't want to be let alone, Clara."

And at that moment the realization of what it would mean to be let alone by this wonderful woman struck him with a leaden force. To be let alone with nothing but the blackness of death before him and the radiant, comforting presence of Clara removed was suddenly intolerable. An atrocious pain seized his heart and entrails.

"Oh, Clara," he exclaimed, "you're not going to leave me?"

"Leave you?" she demanded with a note that struck him as genuine surprise. "How can I leave a man I'm not even with?"

"Then marry me!"

She turned back to the window as if she had not heard him. After a moment, however, she faced him again with a sharp question. "*What* did you say?"

"Marry me. I'll get a divorce. Marry me."

"And become Mrs. Dogcatcher? But no, they won't even run you for *that*."

149

"Oh, Clara, please! What do you want? Blood?"

"I'm not sure. But here we are at my building. No, don't come up. I want to be alone. Good night, Eric!"

◆

Clara the next morning did not go to her office. She knew that her telephone would ring all morning with indignant, if not outraged calls from the party henchmen, and she did not care to have any part of them. All that was over now. She telephoned her friend Polly, who was again in town, this time to visit her ailing mother, and told her that she *had* to lunch with her. Polly was wonderful, as usual. She broke away from the maternal sickbed and came to Clara's house at noon for a drink and a sandwich.

When she heard about Eric's proposal, she raised her glass in a triumphant toast. "Well, it's about time! Cheers for Mrs. Tyler!"

"Don't be so hasty, Polly. Nothing's settled yet. Far from it."

"Oh, you mean about Lucile? She'll sign off, don't worry. Now that the Senate is out the window. Her price will be stiff, but Eric can pay it."

Clara shuddered. "All that is so sordid. The kind of triangular mess I never thought I'd get into. I was going to be myself, lead my own life, with everything fair and square. And now if this divorce gets into the fighting phase, which it surely will, for Lucile will want the moon, I'll be branded in every evening rag as a home breaker and a gold digger. And I'm not even sure I want to marry the man!"

"Oh, Clara, how like you! You've *got* to marry him."

"Why? He's rejected everything I've done for him. He's made a laughingstock of me. Why should I reward his dirty tricks with my lily-white hand?"

"Because he's decided to be a man, that's why, and not just *your* man. Look, my love. I know you like to feel you've accomplished the remarkable things you have accomplished all on your very own. And to a great extent you have. But not quite all, my dear, not quite all. If your nose had been half an inch longer, as they say of Cleopatra, and your ass half a foot wider, would you have had Trevor Hoyt or Eric Tyler at your feet?"

"Oh, Polly, please, not that old argument."

"Why not? Do you deny that we women don't *still* have to use Eve's weapons to get ahead? Maybe in the future we won't have to, but in the here and now, in the second term of the god Eisenhower, if a woman wants to lead in the *real* world — not just the arts and stage but in law firms and corporations and politics — she has to make herself attractive to the ruling sex. And don't pretend that you don't know it!"

"Eric and I have no obligations to each other. We have been entirely candid about that. Either of us is free to break off at will."

"And that's just why you must marry him! Your whole life, your very job, is totally precarious."

"Which is the way I like it."

"Supposing Eric dies. And that son of his takes over. Where will that leave you? Remember how the Hearst boys treated Marion Davies."

"Eric's not going to do any dying for a while."

"How can you say that? He's had heart trouble, hasn't he?"

"He's had fibrillations. I know all about that. He takes something that keeps them entirely under control."

"Well, that's fine, but you never can tell. It's only common sense to prepare for every contingency."

Clara rose to cross the room and stare out the window. She wanted to think, and she didn't care how Polly would interpret her silence. If Polly thought she was considering her financial position in the event of Eric's death, she was welcome to that opinion. It *was* a part of her thinking, but the greater part was her own surprise and shock at facing the fact that her attitude at the prospect of a fatal stroke or heart attack might be bathed in something like detachment.

Was she a monster? Or had his speech at the Waldorf killed her love? And if her feeling for him was so quickly overcome, could it be called love at all? Which raised the question of whether she had ever loved, or even if she could love. And yet maybe what she felt was what everybody felt; maybe it was only the poets and romantics who had blown it up beyond recognition. Surely there was no point reviling herself for feelings or lack of feelings that went on inside herself. Morality had to begin and end in *acts*. No matter what an outdated Bible prescribed.

It was Polly who at last broke the silence. "Do you know something, Clara? If you fail to execute the plan the gods have set up for you, you will be just what you once described Eric to me as being."

Clara turned from the window. "And what is that?"

"A child. A person who plays with life. Someone who's amused to see other people make a mess of things. Well, you'll be amusing yourself seeing yourself make a mess of your own life."

"How am I making a mess of it by simply not marrying one man?"

"Because it's your manifest destiny! Oh God, when I think what *I* could do with your opportunity! Look. You had a plan that you were going to work out *through* Eric. Well, as Mrs. Tyler you'll be able to work it out yourself. You tell me he's desperate to marry you. Doesn't that mean that your influence over him will be greatly increased as a spouse? You know it will! He's going to be anxious to make up to you for the mess he's made of the Senate business. He'll do anything you want. Maybe *you'll* be the one to run for office. I'll bet he'd be proud to back you."

Clara resumed her seat. She found herself intensely interested. "It's perfectly true that he would be far more interested in such a job for me than for himself."

"Ah, but that's just it, don't you see! You would be giving him what he most wants, a front-row seat to view a remarkable career: your own. You both would be happy, and you'd have the life you've always wanted. And someday, we hope in the distant future, when he dies —"

"Polly, don't spoil it," Clara interrupted her anxiously. "You've been doing too well."

"No, no, I must go on. You must see how beautifully I've worked it all out. Someday when Eric dies — as we all shall unless like the Virgin and Saint John the Divine we are allowed a mortal ascent to heaven — he will leave you the bulk of his fortune. He will have provided amply for Lucile and the children in the divorce, and he will want to take full advantage of the marital deduction in his estate tax. And Clarabel Tyler will find herself a famous philanthropist. How I see it all!"

"You see entirely too much."

Clara was now through with the discussion, but when Polly had returned to her mother's bedside, she passed much of the afternoon thinking. Later, when she called Eric and asked to be taken out to dinner, her tone was conciliatory.

13

CLARA ACCOMPANIED ERIC on his visit to the office of Peter Van Alstine, senior partner of the distinguished Wall Street law firm that had represented Eric, and his father before him, for decades. Peter, a portly tweeded gentleman of more than seventy, with tousled gray hair and blinking little almond eyes that combined a mild friendliness with a slumbering suspicion, received them in his great book-lined chamber, which commanded a magnificent view over the harbor and the Statue of Liberty. He seemed surprised, and perhaps not wholly pleased, to see Clara, whom he had met frequently at his client's home and to whom he always behaved with a faintly avuncular courtliness. She assumed, without the least resentment, that the old boy was embarrassed by their relationship.

Eric explained her presence briefly. "Clara is as much concerned with my divorce as I am, Peter. She has honored me with her agreement to become my wife on the first day that is possible, and I want her to take part in all the discussions."

"Which is fine, I am sure," the lawyer replied in a gravelly tone, like a swimmer hurrying over a rocky beach to get to the water. His voice cleared as he warmed to his topic. "Before I submit to you the offer that Lucile has made, on behalf of herself and your children, I think I should place it in the right perspective. They regard it as a final settlement of any claims which any of them may have against you *or* your estate. In other words they would expect nothing more from you either by gift or by will. They also point out that there are no other issues in the proposed divorce proceeding: none of custody of children or division of personalty or alimony. It would be a simple matter of a transfer of capital, after which Lucile would agree to fly to Reno and obtain a virtually automatic divorce."

Eric smiled and winked at Clara. "The proposed settlement must be a hefty one. Let me take a guess at how much they're asking. I must not underestimate Lucile's appetite. Hmm. Half my worldly goods?"

Peter nodded grimly. "The nail on the head."

"But that's an outrage!" Clara exclaimed hotly. "Offer them ten percent and slam the door."

"But, my dear, aren't you forgetting what I'm receiving in return?" Eric asked with a gentle smile to mitigate his playful sarcasm. He reached over to touch her hand, which was resting on the edge of Peter's desk. "Nothing less than yourself."

Clara was not placated. "But I'm not willing to be the price of such extortion. I won't have anything to do with a settlement like that!"

Peter looked from one to another of his clients and then

raised his hands in a plea for a pause. "Please remember that it is only an offer, and presumably not a final one. And your children, Eric, have made a rather unconventional proposal. Tony and Lisa would like to talk to you in front of me, as the old family counsel, without their own lawyer being present, and he has consented to this. They are both waiting in the room next door. Will you see them?"

"My own children? Of course, I'll see them. Clara, you don't mind, do you?"

"No, but perhaps it would be easier if I left."

"I insist that you stay. I may need all your support."

When Tony and Lisa appeared it was immediately evident that Lisa had come only at her brother's insistence. She took a seat farthest from her father and Clara and gazed sullenly out the window. Tony, on the other hand, was tense and active. He went up to his father and briskly shook his hand. But when, to his surprise, Eric reached up to grab his shoulder and pull him down to embrace him, he reddened with pleasure and grinned — even Clara had to admit — almost attractively. He then straightened up and faced the others, glancing obliquely at Clara.

"Perhaps I should preface this meeting by explaining why my mother and her counsel have requested so substantial a settlement. In the first place she takes the position that the Tyler capital is really family money. Although we all recognize Daddy's brilliance in the publishing world" — here he paused to make a little bow to his father — "it is still the case that the money was earned by my grandfather, and it is natural to suppose that he intended it to descend to his posterity."

"If that was his intention, he should have left it in trust," Clara intervened sharply.

"If you would just let me finish, please, Mrs. Hoyt."

"But I'm not admitting your premise!" Clara was irritated by his omission of the more familiar term of address he had used in Eric's office. "He left the property outright to your father to do with as he pleased, and just as he pleased! Or do you suggest that your grandfather didn't understand the difference between an outright bequest and one in trust? Perhaps you are questioning his testamentary capacity?"

"Clara, dear, let him finish," Eric urged her quietly.

"If my mother should reject the divorce," Tony continued now, "and if she should survive Daddy, she would be entitled to one-third of his estate, even if his will left her nothing. So her consent would cost her at least that much, and she feels she cannot ask for less in yielding it. And she has raised the share requested from a third to a half on the theory that she will need the extra amount to make settlements on her children who, after the divorce, may not be able to look to their father for further gifts or bequests."

"Why do you say that, Tony?" Eric asked.

"Because, Dad, you will then be subject to an influence that will not be likely to favor your offspring." With this he stared defiantly at Clara.

She threw back at him: "Do you consider your father a mere puppet?"

"No, but I have a good idea of what he'll be up against."

"If you mean me, say so!"

"Of course I mean you!" As Tony's temper erupted,

Clara took in how deep and savage his resentment of her had to be. For it was not like him to lose all control. "I learned on a safari in Botswana that the most dangerous thing a man can do is to get between a hippo and the water. Well, that's like getting between you and Daddy's dough!"

Clara glanced at Eric. Was the gleam in his eye dismay, or did he, the eternal audience, relish the conflagration that his divorce had sparked? She could not tell. But she decided to strike a different note.

"It's not money for myself that interests me," she pointed out, addressing herself to Peter. "It's what Eric can do with it. You know, he has his own foundation now and is interesting himself more and more in charitable causes. Lucile and the children have already had settlements that should keep them in luxury for the rest of their days. Why does Tony need more money for shiny speedboats and foreign cars or Lisa to endow her future spouses?"

"That's a cheap cut, Clara," Lisa snarled from her corner.

"Can there never be a time for truth?" Clara demanded. "I think a little plain speaking is what we all need."

"And it's plain to see that everything should end up in the lap of the great Mrs. Hoyt!" Tony exclaimed shrilly. "So that she can be the empress of charity!"

Clara rose at this and turned to Eric. "As I suggested earlier, offer them ten percent, take it or leave it. We don't need the divorce. We can go on just the way we are, perfectly well."

Eric also rose. "I think at any rate we should break up

this meeting. I suggest we may all think more clearly if we're less confrontational."

◆

Clara that night had grave reason to suppose that Eric had not derived the amusement she had feared from the hectic scene in the lawyer's office when she was awakened by a telephone call from Eric's butler asking her to come right over. Eric had suffered what appeared to be a mild stroke.

She had ridden with him in the ambulance that had taken him to the hospital and sat for the rest of the night in an armchair by his bed. After a long day of tests he was pronounced out of danger with no permanent damage but a slight impairment of the memory and an occasionally faltering gait. He was allowed to return to his apartment and to go out for a daily airing but at first in a wheelchair. A full recovery was assured him, but his regime had to be carefully monitored.

Clara spent as little time in the Tyler offices as possible and the rest of her days and nights with him. As his doctor forebade any tax on his emotions, she never reverted to the matter of the divorce settlement, and when Tony or Lisa called on their father she silently — and without so much as a nod of greeting — left the room. But one afternoon after the daily tour in Central Park in which she pushed his chair, and during the consumption of the single diluted cocktail that he was now allowed, Eric himself brought up the controversial subject.

"My dear, I have something to tell you. My divorce has been arranged, and Lucile is actually on her way to Reno. If everything goes ahead on schedule, you and I can be married in six weeks' time. That is, of course, if the doctors offer me a decent number of years to live, and you are still willing. I should more than understand if you are not."

"When did all *this* occur?"

"In my talks with Tony."

"And may I ask from where the pound of flesh that he extorted will be taken? Not your poor heart, I hope."

"It's not that bad, my dear. They dropped their demand from a half of all my worldly goods and chattels to a mere third. You are worth far more than that to me!"

"Oh, but I'm not!"

She managed to stifle her cry of dismay. She could not risk it in his condition. By firmly changing the subject, and warning him that he must not get excited, she managed to convey the impression that she would go along with the new arrangement, no matter what her misgivings. But in her lunch the next day with Polly Madison, whose husband was now a vice consul in New York, she exploded.

"The whole thing is so degrading! That a man like Eric should be reduced to crawling before those bloodsuckers who are taking every advantage of his weakened state. And strip himself of one whole third of his wealth to throw it away like all the huge sums they've already got out of him!"

"But, Clara, think of all he has left! You couldn't possibly spend it in a thousand years!"

"Oh, but we could, he and I. It was for the foundation he's set up. One-third of its assets at one fell swoop! How can I marry a man who's capable of such folly? Where's his backbone?"

"Clara! Even you can't be such a fool as that!"

"But think of it, Polly. I was willing to look after him and nurse him and God knows what — to give over my whole life to him if he has another stroke, which the doctors say could happen anytime — and he does *this* to me and all our plans, without so much as a word of warning!"

"Well, it was *his* money, wasn't it? All I can say is that if you throw him over on a flimsy pretext like this, you're a very hard woman to please."

"And why shouldn't I be a hard woman to please? I have only myself to satisfy. Suppose I marry him, and after a year or so Tony and Lisa come around begging for more? Saying they've had losses or expensive ex-spouses to pay or gambling debts — I don't know what. How can I be sure they won't get another giant handout?" Clara was suddenly struck with an idea, and she stared for a long silent moment down at her plate. "Unless I can protect myself with some sort of binding agreement. I've been reading some of those pamphlets on estate planning the bank sends out."

Polly's sigh was a warning. "Oh, my dear, be careful. Men hate women who thrust legal documents at them. They like us at least to pretend we're romantic."

"I can be romantic, Polly. But I need to be a realist first."

"Yes, you *are* a realist. But if I may say so, my friend, you also have a way of cleaning up certain facts that have an aspect not entirely agreeable for you to face."

"For example?"

"Well, don't bite my head off, but I've never quite forgotten how you told me that you were taking nothing from Trevor Hoyt but didn't mention the fact that he had settled a considerable sum on you when you were married."

"Well, would you have had me give *that* up?"

"No, of course not. It was only your attitude. The attitude that you were starting a new life, so to speak, with nothing but your guts and spirit."

Clara looked at her friend now with something close to dislike. "And how do you relate this to me and Eric?"

Polly's embarrassment revealed her regret that she should have given in to the age-old temptation of saying something disagreeable even to her oldest and most useful friend. But she had committed herself now. "I relate it," she replied in a bolder tone, "to my apprehension that you are using your perfectly proper wish to do great and noble things with Eric's money to disguise your equally natural desire to keep it out of the greedy hands of his family."

"But what you really mean is my perfectly natural desire to fill my own pockets!"

Polly shook her head sadly. "Now I've made you mad. I'm sorry. I suggest we've had enough of this. *Parlons d'autre chose.*"

Clara walked up Fifth Avenue after her lunch on her way back to Eric's, determined to dispel her irritation with her friend and to justify to herself her claim to the title of realist. Was she indeed putting the fairest and finest face that she could over her resolution to marry a man she didn't love? But stop right there, she warned herself. What did she mean by not loving him? Had she not loved him before the Senate fiasco? And wasn't love still love when it faded with time? Didn't all love do that? Didn't she like him, as much as she liked anyone in the world? Wasn't that perhaps the way Clara Hoyt loved; might it not be all the love she had in her? People talked such guff about love. The real point was that Eric needed her and was going to need her more, and that she was willing and able to supply his needs. What did people want for a nickel? A nickel? But she was talking about a fortune!

And now a horrid thought struck her, and so sharply, too, that she turned her steps into Central Park and sat down on the first bench on the path. Ah, yes, Clara, she now told herself sharply, but isn't your resolution, and your good will, as well, founded on your inner suspicion that the period of their testing may not be too prolonged? That Eric may die? The pain of this was a stabbing one, and she jumped up to relieve it and resume her walk. There had to be a truce to so much introspection! Had she created herself? Was she responsible for the stream of her own consciousness? Or of her unconsciousness? Life had to go on.

She was relieved to find Eric out of his wheelchair and even nattily dressed. He seemed suddenly almost his old self again when he suggested a game of backgammon, and they settled themselves before the board. But when she had won the first play and had placed her cup with the dice upside down on the table she did not pick it up.

"Wait," she said firmly. "I want to talk first about our marriage."

"Fine."

"I've said I'll always be square with you, and I will be. But I must protect you and myself from further demands from your grasping family. Some might say, by out-grasping them. Very well. I'll do just that. I agree to marry you and to look after you for the rest of your life or of my own, whichever is the shorter ——"

"But, Clara dear, I've never asked for any such thing!"

"I know that. But in view of what I'm asking I want you to know what I'm offering."

"You mean as a quid pro quo?"

"You might put it that way, if you like."

"Ah, my dear, as to what *I* like!"

"Anyway, here it is. I want you to give a quarter of your estate now to your foundation." She paused. "And put all the rest in an irrevocable trust, with income to yourself for life. Plus a power, of course, to invade the principal for emergencies."

Eric was following her carefully now. "For emergencies?"

"Oh, you know, health, mental incompetence and so on. In the discretion of the trustees. With an income as large as yours it's a power that would probably never be exercised."

"I see. And on my death?"

"On your death half the principal of the trust would go to your foundation. The other half would be held in further trust and the income paid to your widow for her life."

"That presumably would be you."

"Well, you can't imagine that I've planned all this for Lucile, can you?"

"Hardly. And on my widow's demise?"

"The principal would go to your foundation. Thus everything you have would end up eventually in *your* foundation. Because there would be no estate tax, thanks to the marital deduction."

"Very clever, indeed. You've been talking to a lawyer?"

"No, but I've read some of those bank pamphlets."

"Then you must have learned that to qualify for the deduction I must give you the power to appoint the principal of your trust by will to anyone you like."

"And cut out the foundation?"

"Just so. My widow, for example, might be tempted to exercise the power in favor of her child by a previous marriage."

Clara looked at him carefully. He was smiling; he was playing with her, but he was also serious. "You mean I might leave it all to Sandra? She'll have plenty of Hoyt money, and besides, she's already very anti—big fortune. But I'd be willing to give you my word that the power would never be exercised. I assume that would be enough?"

"You assume correctly." His nod seemed decisive. "And I think the plan is a good one. The only thing I can think of adding at the moment is that I want to make you chairman of the trustees of my foundation."

"Oh, Eric, *you* must be that!"

"I shall sit on the board, yes. But I want you to be chairman. After all, you will be, one day, and you may as well start now." At this his expression grew grave. "There is, however, one question that I want to put to you before I call in Van Alstine. Tell me truly, Clara, do you still love me?" Then he shook his head, as if impatiently. "No, let me change that. Do you love me?"

"Of course, I love you."

"Could you repeat that, leaving out the 'of course'?"

"I love you, Eric."

He gave a little clap with his hands. "The deed of gift to the foundation and the trust will be drawn up this week. They shouldn't take long. I could draft them myself, if necessary. And we can be married as soon as Lucile's decree comes through. I had said that we'd need a doctor's okay, but the way I'm feeling now I have no doubt that we'll get it! Shall we go on with our game?"

Clara lifted her cup. It was absurd; it was even ironic; worse than both, it was grotesque. She had rolled double sixes!

In the days that followed she was haunted by the thought that she had lied to him for the first and only time. But was it really a lie? She kept reassuring herself with the arguments she had used on the bench in Central Park. Was it a lie to deny a purely subjective state of mind? Was it wrong to hoist the banner of the state of mind one *wanted* to have, the state of mind that one was determined to live by and up to? What *business* was it of anyone else's, even of the man one was going to marry? None!

14

ON THE DAY AFTER LUCILE TYLER received her decree in Reno, Eric and Clara were married in the office of Peter Van Alstine by a judge of the New York Court of Appeals, an old friend and college classmate of the groom. Sandra did not attend but not because she disapproved. She accepted Eric as a stepfather with the same mild but faintly enigmatic good manners with which she had accepted him as her mother's companion. "I'll see you when you get home" was all she said.

Eric owned a small ranch near Phoenix, Arizona, and in view of the state of his health Clara had decided that they would pass a quiet and solitary honeymoon there. Eric slept during most of the flight out on a chartered plane while she skimmed over some applications to the Tyler Foundation, which already, due to the rapidly spreading news of his recent major grant, were beginning to pour in.

She had thought they might discuss one of the more interesting of these at the ranch, but Eric was too tired to do much more than sit in an armchair on the terrace and bask in the winter sun. His mood was subdued but amiable and apparently content; sometimes, when she was sitting by him reading, he would reach over to take her hand and hold it for a moment in silence.

One day at noontime he asked her surprisingly: "Isn't it odd how peaceful it is here?"

"Why should it be odd?"

"Because the desert is so full of hostility. Haven't you noticed? Everything is ready to bite or prick you. Yet the overall effect is curiously benign. I was thinking it's not unlike death. Life is full of pricks and bites, and yet beyond them all — or really perhaps around them all, *in* them all — is peace."

"I had hoped you would find your life, at least on our honeymoon, less threatened."

"Well, you've certainly done everything you could to make it less so, my dear. And anyway, let's hope that nothing as intrusive as death, whenever and however it occurs, will interrupt our honeymoon. Everyone would suppose it had come from too much ardor for my weakened frame. Whereas, alas, the very opposite is true."

"Never fear. There'll be plenty of time for ardor when you're well again."

"And in the meantime, if you spot a handsome cowboy, trust me to look the other way."

"If you keep talking like that, I'll do it in front of you!"

"Ah, how true! You always said I was a voyeur."

The houseboy interrupted their persiflage with Eric's one permitted drink and Clara's gin fizz. "Tell me," she said when the boy had gone, "what has been pricking you. For I don't suppose it's just the scorpions and cacti that have brought on this mood."

"To tell you the truth, I've been a bit worried about Tony. Lisa's settlement was in trust, of course, but his was outright."

Clara scowled into her glass. Would they never be free of the wretched Tony? "Well, he wanted it that way, didn't he?"

"Very much so. Too much so. That's just the point. That may be why I should have protected him."

"Against what? Wine, women and song? They're hardly Tony's problem."

"No, against himself. That right-wing sheet of his has got itself into bad trouble with libel suits, and he's been pouring money into it. Big money, I'm afraid."

"Well, isn't that his lookout? If worst comes to worse, he can always look to his mother."

"Lucile considers herself allergic to giving. Though how she knows it, we can't guess. She's never tried."

"Anyway it's out of your hands, and thank heaven for that. If Tony needs protection against himself, you need it against *him!* And your trust is it."

"I still have the income."

Clara could not restrain her impatience now. "Yes, and if you want to give it all to him, go ahead and do so! But don't tell me about it!"

"I'm sorry, my dear. Please don't get so upset. I have no idea of giving all my income to Tony, or even any considerable slice of it. But there is one thing you could do for me. It troubles me to think how Tony will feel when I go to my reward, or my punishment, whichever it may be, and he finds that he has no share of my estate."

"But he knows that, Eric! He waived all that!"

"He might think that I'd held back some share, however slight, to bequeath to him. My only son! How humiliating for him to read in the newspapers that he's been disinherited! For they'll never mention what I've already given him."

"And what am I expected to do about that? For my share is all in trust, too, you know."

"You can put him on the board of the foundation. And tell him it was my last wish. That will be something, at least. A Tyler son on the Tyler Foundation. It will give him a kind of status. And show him that I still cared."

"Oh, Eric!" she wailed.

"Promise me just that."

After a long pause, she nodded, her eyes angrily closed. "Very well. I promise."

"Thank you, my love."

Eric's second stroke felled him soon after their arrival back in New York. He was taken to the hospital, where he lingered for two days in a coma. And on the third the new Mrs. Tyler became his widow.

Clara went through the motions of arranging and attending his large funeral in what struck her as a kind of trance. The relatives, even his children, behaved to her with a hushed formality that required few words and few reactions. His old secretary, stricken but controlled, took most of the details of the service off her hands, and the old butler handled the big buffet lunch that followed it at Eric's apartment with his habitual skill. It seemed to Clara that the etiquette of death provided a blessedly civilized interlude between the end of one life and the resumption of another. Sorrow, expectations, hope and even remorse could wait, relegated to the corners of the dark room whose very emptiness offered her a kind of relief. Even her mother, even Polly, did little more than silently hug her.

It was on the second morning after the funeral, having breakfast with Sandra, that Clara first felt reality peeping into that vacant chamber of her fantasy. Sandra was now sixteen, with lovely dark hair and a pale, handsome, thoughtful countenance. She was never going to rival her mother in looks, Clara fully realized, but she would do well enough in the soberer role for which she was fitted. Mother and daughter had never been intimate, but their quarrels, however sharp, had been soon patched up. It was as if each faced an inward sense that they had to get on together.

Clara wondered now if the girl hated her. She had always followed a rigid rule of never openly cultivating Sandra's affection, never trying to break her down by a flurry of hugs or kisses, or even by a display of maternal sobs. What would come must come of its own.

"Do you want me to wear a mourning band on my sleeve when I go to school?" Sandra asked. "Some girls do."

"Do you want to?"

"Well, most girls don't, usually. But I will if you want me to."

"Thank you, dear, but no, I don't want you to at all. I doubt if I'll even wear black myself, except maybe for a week or so. One of the purposes of mourning attire was that it was supposed to stop people who didn't know from asking embarrassing questions, but everyone I know is well aware that Eric is dead. And for you, it isn't as if he had been your father. Do you think you'll miss him?"

"Oh, yes. He was always so nice to me. And bought me so many lovely things, though I know you shouldn't count that in caring for a person. But I suppose one does, doesn't one?"

"Oh, one can't help but count it! And think of all the lovely things he bought *me*."

"Will *you* miss him, Mother?"

Clara tried not to look startled. The question was important. Was the girl challenging her at last? Challenging her openly for the first time?

"What makes you think I wouldn't, darling?"

"Oh, simply that you live so much in the present. Daddy says you live more in the present than anyone he's ever known."

Ah, she was deep, the girl! Deep enough to disguise any hostility behind the veil of polite discussion.

"Well, it's the most practical place to live, isn't it? What else did Daddy say about me?"

"He says now you'll be rich. Very rich. That's true, isn't it?"

"Yes, it's true. I'll be able to do things for people. People who need it. It will be a great challenge."

Sandra's silence seemed to contemplate a less philanthropic use of her mother's new resources. But she wasn't going to say it. Not a word! What she did say was very different. "Daddy was afraid it might be hard on you."

"Riches? Why? I know they're not meant to bring happiness, but they don't have to bring unhappiness, do they?"

"He said there were three things the possession of any one of which could make people hate you. And that you have all three!"

"Heavens! And what are those three things?"

"Wealth, power and beauty."

Clara gasped. "Well, thank him anyway for the beauty! I guess he hasn't seen me for a while."

"Oh, yes, he saw you at the funeral."

"Really? He came to that?"

"He did. He said Eric had always been good to me. And he took me home when you had to go to the interment."

"That was very dear of him." But she didn't somehow quite like it. It was as if her old life were joining with the rest of her world in a tribute to a man which mysteriously excluded her. "Anyway, to answer your question, of course, I shall miss Eric. But I shall have the sense of his being with me, working at the foundation on all the things he and I cared about."

It rang false, and she felt sure that Sandra took it so. But it didn't matter. There had to be a base on which they could settle things, and what base was there that contained no alloy at all?

"Will the foundation be in Eric's old office?"

Clara welcomed the switch to detail. "For the time being, I suppose. But it will be a bigger proposition now. It will eventually need its own quarters."

Sandra nodded and rose to get ready for school. In the following days she made no further reference to the man who had been so briefly her stepfather, but her deportment to her mother was unexceptional.

A great deal of Clara's time in the next weeks had to be spent in the not unwelcome distraction of the administration of her husband's estate, and her visits to Peter Van Alstine's office were frequent and prolonged. She was determined to dispose of most of the periodicals, keeping a couple of favorites, so that she could devote most of her time to the foundation, but she was in no hurry, and the same caution would be used in the sale of Eric's various residences. Her own houses in town and country would do well enough for her, and she would pick what she wanted from his art collection and auction the rest.

"And the children?" Peter inquired. "Nothing for them?"

"They can have what they want, within reason," she replied with a shrug. "But they're going to have to come to me and ask. Neither Tony nor Lisa has been near me since the funeral. What are they hatching? Have you heard?"

"The silence may be ominous. I know Tony's been seeing Irving Sayles."

"Who's he? Some shyster?"

"Far from it, Clara. He's the big litigator who broke the Murphy will."

It was only another week before Sayles fired his first round. Representing what he dramatically described as "the shorn next of kin," his petition on behalf of Eric's two children alleged an "infamous" conspiracy between the decedent's treacherous counsel and his designing widow to deflect his entire estate from his natural heirs. Tyler, it was affirmed, had been reduced to a state of childishness by his stroke and isolated from his family and associates so that his feeble willpower could be more effectively worked on. And in the execution of the fatal deed of gift in trust, his "paramour" — not yet his lawful spouse — was said to have virtually guided his trembling hand.

"What puzzles me about this petition," Peter told Clara as they went over it, "is the violence of the language. That's not like Irving. After all, it's got to be a strike suit, looking for an early and advantageous settlement. They must know that Eric was of perfectly sound mind and that they can't prove any of this garbage. Why get our backs up so that we might rather die than settle for a penny?"

"Because Tony cares more about splattering me with mud than he does about the money itself!"

Peter shook his head in rumination. "He must have paid old Irving a whopping retainer to make him go against his better judgment like this."

"Good! You mean that old Irving isn't taking the case on a purely contingent basis?"

"No, that's not his way. He wants his hourly stipend."

"Then let's bust Tony, Peter! We're sure to win the case, aren't we? Oh, I know you lawyers always say that no case is a sure bet, but this is as near a one as possible, isn't it?"

"Well, I'd say it's twenty to one in our favor, yes. There's always the chance of some quack medical testimony and a crazy jury."

"Then can't we drag it out?" Clara suggested eagerly. "Can't we look as if we were just about to crumble and then start up again? Can't we keep suggesting settlements and then withdrawing them? I don't care if we litigate for *years!* If we can only bust Tony with his legal fees. And don't worry about yours! I'll pay them whatever they are!"

Peter held up his hands in dismay. "Clara, Clara, my dear, you're asking *me* to be a shyster. And think what you yourself would be going through. Think of the publicity!"

"Oh, I don't give a hoot about that! If Tony thinks I'm going to mind a bad press, he forgets that I've been in that game for years."

"Then must I remind you, as a realist, that if the contestants ask for a settlement that would cost you less than a protracted legal battle it might be your duty, both as executrix and foundation president, to settle it."

"You mean that I have no moral right to protect my own reputation? I'll take that issue, sir, to the highest court in the land!" She felt a sudden exaltation as she spoke. This was the note to strike! She was now on the side of the angels. She might in her heart even find it possible to be grateful to Tony!

"Well, let us see what comes of it. Maybe I can move for a directed verdict after they state their case."

Peter ended their interview with the complacent nod of the old lawyer who has heard so many brave words, all too many times before. Clara understood what he was thinking: that like so many volatile female clients she could be made to see reason in the end. But he would find out!

And as the months dragged on he did find out. The contestants were very persistent. Their counsel dragged every lawyer and secretary and accountant in Eric's office who had ever worked on a Tyler matter to the stand, and every servant who had ever served in the Tyler household. They had Clara in the witness box for hours, but she never flinched or hesitated in her bold clear testimony. One journalist even observed that she seemed to be enjoying herself.

At last the stubborn Tony appeared to have been persuaded by his weary counsel to submit to settlement, and the offers began to creep in. The contestants kept lowering the figure demanded. No longer did they insist on half the residuary estate, or even a third, or a tenth . . .

At last an offer was received that would do little more, in Peter's shrewd estimate, than compensate Tony's counsel for all their violent forensic efforts. He wrote the sum on a slip of paper and handed it silently across his desk for Clara to see.

She glanced at it and then up at the wrinkled brown face before her, furrowed as it seemed with decades of calming down impetuous clients, pleading against their hasty and unruly judgments, draining the emotions out of their lives to leave the dark sediment of common sense. She took in the tousled gray hair, disarrayed by the life-long scratching of his scalp over human folly and the blinking little almond eyes that could peer into every crack and corner in search of compromise.

When he spoke it was to anticipate her objection.

"If you could only bring yourself, my dear, to view the matter in the light of which will cost Eric's estate the least — to pay this sum or go on with the fight — it would make things much simpler."

"But that is not at all the way I see it. Tony has held me up to the world as a brazen and shameless hussy. And Tony is going to pay for it!"

"But all that was just the usual language of will contests. Everyone knows it means nothing. Nobody in their right mind today thinks that an advantageous settlement is an admission of charges. They know what the costs of litigation are."

"Peter, there is no point in your even submitting to me

another offer of compromise. I tell you here and now that I won't settle for a penny!"

She looked again at the paper in her hand. If that were indeed what Tony would have to pay his counsel, it was a thumping sum, and she felt an exhilaration in her heart. But as she watched her old lawyer, shaking his head mournfully as he turned back to the pile of papers beside him and plucked one out, apparently for further discussion, she had a sudden misgiving. Was she whitewashing herself with the heavily splashed paint of her lofty stand? In so sternly rejecting the very possibility that there could be the smallest validity in her stepson's charges, was she desperately affirming her own virtue to herself? Even buying it with what was still a substantial sum of money?

"I must bring to your attention, Clara, that there is another aspect to this proposed settlement. It can be arranged at no cost to you personally. Eric's sister, Miss Tyler, who, as you know, is an officer of his foundation and who has taken your side consistently in this litigation, has approached me with the suggestion that the foundation make the payment to the contestants and that no part of it be charged to your trust. She completely understands that you wish to have nothing to do with any settlement with the contestants who have so wrongfully aspersed you, but she feels that it is to the economic advantage of the foundation to settle and that its officers should not be swayed by personal resentment. She has also informed me that a majority of the foundation's five trustees agree with her."

"But not I! Not the president!"

"I'm afraid the president can be outvoted. It's four to one, Clara."

Clara drew herself up. She had anticipated this. "Then tell my sister-in-law, and the others — of whom you are one, Peter, dear old traitor that you are — that if one penny of the foundation's assets is paid either to Eric's children *or* their counsel by way of settlement of their false claims, I shall execute a will in which I exercise the power of appointment, given me by my husband, to direct that on my death the principal of my trust shall pass to a beneficiary or beneficiaries *other* than the foundation."

Peter gaped. "You would defeat Eric's plan?"

"And do so with the knowledge that he would totally approve!"

"But you gave him your word, Clara!"

"And now I take it back! Do you doubt me, Peter?"

"Oh, no." For a moment he simply scratched his brow. "No, I do not do that. Very well, I must tell Miss Tyler that the offer must be rejected. For of course no foundation could risk the loss of a principal that would double it in size for the relatively minor sum that the continuation of this futile suit would cost it. So there we are! At least, my dear, you have been consistent."

15

PETER VAN ALSTINE declined to implement Clara's plan of spinning out the defense of the suit in order to expand the contestants' costs. His litigating partner conducted the case with efficiency and dispatch, asking and receiving a directed verdict for the executors as soon as he had finished cross-examining the last witness called by the plaintiffs' counsel to sustain their flimsy cause. Tony appealed desperately and unsuccessfully to the Appellate Division and was stuck, as Clara had ardently hoped, with big fees. It was total victory.

And this was only the prelude to better things: two years of what seemed to the radiant Clara to be a kind of apotheosis of herself. The press appeared to be intent on making her a symbol of female glamor and power in the era of waxing women's rights that characterized Ike's second term. She was seen as the angel of beneficence, photographed in the new offices of the Tyler Foundation in a new Fifth Avenue tower against an entrance foyer with a small reflecting pool or a conference chamber adorned with Eric's collection of Gauguin Tahitian scenes. If her picture failed to appear any Sunday in the *Times*'s account of parties of the week, her friends joked, they would call up to ask if she was ill.

The board of the foundation consisted, initially, of only five persons: herself, as the all-powerful chairman; Peter Van Alstine; Polly Madison; the now retired Albany judge who had married her and Eric; and her sister-in-law, Miss Elmina Tyler. Clara had at once established as the goals of the foundation the support of the liberal arts in museums, colleges and theatres, which meant that every hour of the considerable workday that she was happy to put in would be not only interesting but amusing. She appointed the compliant art critic whom she had already hired for *Style* as executive director and gave him a staff of six. Only Miss Tyler offered her any trouble at all, and that was very mild.

Elmina Tyler was a robust, mannish, goodhearted woman, with a square red face and bobbed gray hair, who made no effort to be anything but the bluff, down-to-earth creature that she appeared. She was what her generation called "horsey," and indeed she ran a small stud farm in northern New Jersey. If she had lesbian inclinations she kept them well out of sight. Clara had found her as easy to win over as Eric's secretary, Annie Hally; Elmina had been sincerely fond of her brother and had sensibly seen that Clara was a far better mate for him than any of his earlier lady friends. She had little interest in the arts, but she was faithful in her attendance at board meetings and paid close attention to the discussions. When she introduced propositions of her own, unrelated to the stated goals of the institution, such as saving the wolves or the rain forests, Clara could usually satisfy her with a relatively small grant. But there was one subject on which their disagreement was not so easily settled.

"I'm well aware that Tony has treated you shamefully," Elmina told her, "and I've certainly let him know it. But a lot of that was attributable to his lawyers. You know how they get when they sink their teeth into a lawsuit! Tony has had some hard knocks recently, but I believe he's learned his lesson. And I think it's a sad thing that a son of Eric's hasn't a seat on the board of his foundation."

"Even a son who publicly asserted that his father was of unsound mind and putty in the hands of a designing woman?"

"But, Clara, that was just legal gobbledygook!"

"When a person throws that much mud, Elmina, some of it is bound to stick."

"But not forever!"

"Well, for a while. Longer than we've had, anyway."

Miss Tyler nodded to indicate her acceptance that this short round was over. "I'll bring it up again next year."

Clara's favorite beneficiary and the source of her greatest interest was the New York colossus, the Museum of World Art, on whose stellar board she had taken Eric's old place. It was not long after her first major grant to that institution that its president wisely promoted her to the Acquisitions Committee, and there she formed a delightful friendship with Oliver Kip, the curator of Italian painting, whose brilliantly convincing presentations to the members had aroused the jealous indignation of the other department heads who feared an imbalance in moneys appropriated for the purchase of artifacts.

Clara was perfectly aware that Kip was concentrating his particular charm on herself, for he was too smart to be unaware that even if the Acquisitions Committee outvoted Mrs. Tyler in the proposed purchase of an object that he coveted she might well arrange for her foundation to buy it. But Kip's charm was such that she had no objection to being its victim. After all, everyone conceded that he was an expert in the Italian Renaissance. His record in the objects he had acquired for the museum was without a stain.

He was a bachelor, apparently a couple of years her junior; he admitted, perhaps not quite truthfully, to thirty-seven. He was a bit on the short side and just the tiniest bit plump, but he was agile and possessed of a catlike grace in all his movements, debonair in his courtliness, with smooth skin and thick curly brown hair pulled straight back from a broad pale cerebral brow, a fine aristocratic nose, thin tight lips and eyes of a serenely questioning blue.

He took her on guided tours of the museum, and not just his own department but all the others; he seemed to be as familiar with Roman or Greek art as with Italian, and his knowledge even embraced primitive Africa. He was vivid but at the same time concise and to the point. Whether he was telling her the story of a grand duchess, painted by Vigée-Lebrun on her visit to Saint Petersburg, or Gauguin's liaison with a Tahitian woman, or how Philippe de Champaigne had to express the human body in robes because his Jansenism forbade him to paint the nude, he wove art and history into a tapestry of delight.

The first social occasion to which he invited her was a dinner for eight that he was giving for the president of the museum and his wife. His apartment was small but as exquisite as she had expected. His passion for the Italian Renaissance had not included its rather massive furniture or its heavy porcelain; it was represented only by his collection of master drawings on the walls. The rest was drawn from the elegance of the Venetian eighteenth century: delicately wrought chairs upholstered in yellow silk, consoles with gilded animal legs, mirrors of stained glass in intricately carved frames. And in the air a faint odor of incense.

Oliver was carefully turning the pages of a huge album spread out on a table to show Clara and another early arrival his finest drawings, kept there and not hung to avoid sunlight, when she suddenly caught his hand with an exclamation of excitement.

"Oh, wait, let me look longer at this one!"

"Trust you, Clara, to pick my prize," he said with a smile. "It's Rembrandt."

The drawing depicted Christ returning from the Mount of Olives to find the three disciples, whom he had asked to keep watch, fast asleep. A mere dozen or so masterstrokes had sufficed to endow the face and upheld hands of Jesus with a wonderful sense of sorrow, acceptance and love, tinged with a foreboding of the doom that awaited him.

"The brown wash on the trees in the background may have been added by another hand," Oliver suggested. "But it doesn't hurt the overall effect."

"Where on earth did you get such a marvel?" she asked.

But Oliver caught sight now of a couple entering the

room and he abruptly closed the album. "Here is our president. We must not show him too many treasures."

"Why? Did you filch them? I could hardly blame you."

"No. A sharp eye can make up for a thin purse. But we
must not arouse his envy."

On her next visit to the museum she wanted to see all
the Rembrandt drawings in the collection, to compare
them with his, and, meeting her in the great hall to guide
her to the storage rooms, they passed through the Greek
and Roman galleries. He could never, however, withold a
passing comment, and he paused to show her the base of a
column taken from a Roman edifice in Caesarea. On it
was inscribed a date and part of the letters in the name
and title of Pontius Pilate, Procurator.

"You see before you," he announced gravely, "a most
significant window into the past. No other contemporary
archeological, epigraphic or numismatic evidence exists
that the judge of Jesus ever lived."

"What about the Gospels?"

"All written later. They might be as fictional as Anatole
France's delightful story of the aged Pilate, retired to a
villa on the Bay of Naples, who cannot even recall the
name of the Jewish thaumaturgist whom he delivered to
the mob."

"You mean Christ himself might not have existed?"

"Oh, I don't say that. I simply point out how slender the
evidence is. All hearsay that would be excluded by any
court of law. That is why I cling to this pedestal. Pilate, at
least, existed. And out of that I can deduce the whole New
Testament, the way a dinosaur can be deduced from a single bone in its toe."

"You mean that from Pilate you can deduce the Crucifixion?"

"Just so. For had Pilate spared him, Jesus would have done himself in by continuing to preach, right into his old age, the imminent destruction of the world that never came."

"You sound like Gibbon. Are you even a Christian, Oliver?"

"You mean do I believe in all the horrors of the early church? The persecutions, the burnings, the relic hunting, the theological split hairs, the idiotic Crusades? I should hope not! In history I skip directly from the Greeks to Leonardo!"

"Using your pedestal as a steppingstone?"

Going to art galleries with Oliver was even more exciting. Seated with him in a private back room after the dealer had brought out the work of art requested and placed it on a table or easel before them and then discreetly retired — Kip could not endure the presence of a chattering salesman while he studied an artifact — Clara would silently wait for his first comment. She could always tell when he wanted to acquire something for the museum, for he seemed to turn into a different person. His voice would become tense and sharp; he would make no effort to persuade or dazzle or coax her as a potential donor. Oh, no, he was suddenly above all that. He seemed to be sternly offering her the choice of damning herself forever as a hopeless philistine or just managing to squeeze through the closing gates of the angels. She was a bit afraid of this second Oliver Kip.

The second Oliver was very much in evidence one

morning when they were at the Lecky Gallery examining the small portrait of a young man, apparently a Florentine, seen in profile, head and shoulders, against a background of blue hills and a silvery winding road on which two men in armor were riding a black and a white steed. The youth, brilliantly handsome, was wearing a red cap over his finely curled raven locks and a pleated red doublet over a black tunic. Clean-shaven, his features were strong and pale, and his eye, bold and piercing, had yet in it what seemed to signify something more than intelligence, perhaps even a rare sensitivity.

Oliver had been silent so long that at last she asked: "Who is he? Do we know?"

"Perhaps a member of the Strozzi family."

"And the painter?"

"They're not sure. It could be Ghirlandaio. A painter absurdly underestimated by Berenson. Or his workshop. But I seem to make out the master's touch. Although the date's a little late for him. You can read it on the cornice over the subject's head. 1492."

"The year Columbus sailed the ocean blue!"

"But rather, for us Renaissance lovers, the year France invaded Italy and started the whole bloody occupation that, with Spain to help, stamped out the light of civilization."

"Forever?"

"Well, have we really had any since then? Before the Renaissance, men looked for God in the sky. Since the Renaissance, they've looked for God in other men: Napoleon, Lincoln, Hitler, Stalin, what have you. But in the Renaissance, men looked for God in themselves. Consider this wonderful young Strozzi, or whoever he is. He doesn't trouble himself with visions of heaven or hell or dream up ideal societies to make the miserable creatures around him more miserable than they already are. He will settle for the one life he has and make it a beautiful thing!"

But Clara wasn't going to let him ride roughshod over her. "So to hell with everyone else? The only time to live was the Renaissance? What about all the people they poisoned? What about that poor clumsy page in the Symonds book you gave me whom one of Cesare Borgia's officers punished by pushing him into the fireplace and holding him there with a poker until he was burned to a crisp? Was that so beautiful?"

Oliver looked at her with a surprised exasperation. "Really, Clara, what sort of argument is that? There are brutes in every era."

"And Machiavelli? You approve of his cynicism?"

"His principles guide every statesman today. It's no longer fashionable to admit them, that's all."

She decided she had gone far enough. There was one sure way to change him back to the other Oliver Kip. "Well, I give up. I never heard such an existentialist. And do you know something? You look very much like your Strozzi. Isn't that a sufficient reason for my recommending its purchase by the Tyler Foundation?"

His smile was now radiant. "Clara, you're a darling! And a shrewd eye, to boot. For that portrait is a steal if it's a true Ghirlandaio, and I think I'll be able to prove it is! But hush!" And he glanced around conspiratorially in mock fear of being overheard by a salesman with an ear to a keyhole.

The purchase of the Florentine youth by a grant from the Tyler Foundation marked a new stage in their friendship. Oliver was less deferentially polite with her now; he seemed to regard her more as a partner than either a trustee of his employer or a pupil of his own. There was a kind of intimacy in the way he explained things to her that she found at first titillating and then pleasantly erotic. It was beginning to be clear to what their relationship was tending.

She was now much more aware of him physically. Having been brought up in France by expatriate parents, Oliver manipulated his body and limbs with the coordinated grace of a perfect Gallic gentleman. His every move and gesture was confined to its purpose with a seamless efficiency. If he opened a door and stepped aside for her to enter first, if he got into a taxi before her so that she wouldn't have to climb into the farther seat, if he stooped in a restaurant to retrieve a napkin she had dropped, he lent charm to his action. She had a sense that this man would never indulge in anything so vulgar as foreplay, that when the moment came for sexual union it would be accomplished as easily and effectively as any other demonstration of bodily activity, as if indeed to show that all other such had been his own method of foreplay.

As the notion that they were about to become lovers took firm hold in her mind, it was accompanied by a sudden wakening of her senses stronger than that evoked by any other man in her life, including her long forgotten first fiancé with the crew cut and broad shoulders. Stronger but very different. She wanted to belong to Oliver, to be appreciated by his cool, appraising eyes, to be added to his collection of beautiful objects. She didn't even seem to care very much about the state of his heart, whether or not he loved her in a romantic sense. Could Oliver love? Did she even want him to? She knew only that she wanted him.

And when it happened it was, unlike most such encounters in life, very much what she had fantasized. They had been to a gallery to inspect a show of paintings of French interiors by Walter Gay, an American expatriate of the belle époque who had specialized in depicting the elegant rooms of his own and his friends' chateaux. The Museum of World Art had lent one of these, and Oliver wished to see if it was properly displayed.

"Did Gay never put people in his rooms?" Clara asked after they had made their tour of the gallery. "Why are they always empty?"

"Oh, I think he did when he was young. But for some reason after middle age he banned the human figure. One theory is that he was so bored by the stylish set that flooded these chambers, that he shooed them all away, like Christ and the money changers."

Clara paused before the study of a little foyer with a marble parquet floor and french doors opening on a garden. "Maybe Gay was thinking of the people who *should* have occupied these rooms. Charming people, of course! Can't you just see the couple who walked through those doors into that lovely garden? Only a few minutes ago? Beautiful! That might have been his way of doing their portraits!"

Oliver smiled. "That is real beauty, then? What you *don't* see?"

When they walked up Park Avenue afterwards and came to his building, he paused.

"Will you come up, my dear?" he asked her in a tone that was suddenly serious, almost grave. "I should like you to see my apartment."

"But, Oliver, what are you talking about? You know I've seen it!"

"Ah, but only with others."

"You mean I must see it empty? Like a Walter Gay?"

"You must see it with just me. And the best room you haven't seen at all."

Which was her introduction to his gilded Venetian bedroom with the wide-canopied bed and the sculpted angels over the bedstead. But before he made love to her he made a request that thrilled her as much as it surprised her. He asked her if she would pose for a sketch in the nude. When she had disrobed and settled herself on the bed in the pose of Goya's *Maja Desnuda,* he, still fully clothed, sat down to work on his drawing in utter silence for some twenty minutes. It had the effect of perfectly preparing her for what was to follow. It made her feel that her exposure was the most natural thing in the world, even a kind of professional exercise, and it dispelled any shrinking fear that her body, no longer young, might fail to please him. It also put him in a position of male mastery that more than balanced any consideration of her being the rich patroness of his employer. If she was a goddess, she had nonetheless stripped to submit herself to the judgment of Paris.

16

TONY TYLER had learned, more or less, to live with his multifold resentments. He had a way of dressing them up and marching them up and down the inner stage of his turbulent thoughts. This habit had been impressed upon him early in life, by watching his cool and rarely ruffled mother, in whose custody he had been largely reared, and noting that she was apt to get her way by not allowing her contempt for the world too visibly to erupt. Oh, she let it be suspected, all right! A faint smoke was discernible over the crater of her by no means extinct volcano. But her stately saunter past the respectful throng of her severely limited society put him in mind of a beautiful black and white skunk sporting over its sleek back a fine, bushy tail. Tony himself, however, lacking both her beauty and her stateliness, had had to make gestures to appease the world. His trouble was that he couldn't seem to hide what he was trying to do. People suspected a concealed hostility and wondered what it was based upon.

He had never been able to achieve in any activity a first position, or at least what he regarded as that. At school the slightness of his build had relegated him to only a second or third place in sports, and what one could only rate as the slightness of his intellect (despite a perfect memory, at least for snubs) had kept him in the second rank of scholarship. Finally, he had been mocked as a boy — oh, bitter memory! — for the slightness of his private parts, though these had later developed normally, and it might have been that which had long hampered him in social life and kept him, until college age, on the outer circle of even friendly groups. But worst of all was his constant sense of falling below the standards of his parents. His mother used her beauty and regal composure and absolute self-assurance to dominate the small part of the world that she valued, and his father conquered the rest of it with his easy charm, his wit and his athletic prowess. It had given Tony a fierce little inner satisfaction that they had so evidently disliked each other. Their marriage, at least, had been a total failure!

And his own? Aye, there had been the rub. His own should have been a shining example to them of all they had missed. And instead he found himself wed to a woman who had been permanently disillusioned by her discovery that he was not the man she had thought he was. He had, of course, been scared of being married for his money, and now he almost wished that he had been. He had made the mistake of proposing to a lovely and unworldly girl, a Long Island neighbor and childhood friend of his sister, who was just recovering from an infatuation with the lifeguard at their beach club who had ditched her for an heiress. She had turned in her desperation to the familiar Tony, professing to see in his reserve, modesty; in his hesitation, scrupulous honesty; and in his doubts and apprehensions, a search for truth. Annette was too honest to blame her husband for her crude misconceptions, but he held against her that she witheld her admiration, and he saw in her passionate devotion to the twin daughters that were born of their match a certain repudiation of himself.

Nor did it help matters that she had been disgusted by his lawsuit against his father's estate.

"Why can't you accept the will?" she had demanded. "Your dad settled more than enough on you. It wasn't his fault that you piddled away half of it on that fascist sheet of yours. And you know that he wasn't any more subject to undue influence from Clara than you are from me!"

"I deny that!"

"Oh, pooh. If you get any sort of settlement out of it, it'll be nothing but extortion. And if I ever get my paws on a penny of it, I'll turn it right back to Clara!"

"I'll certainly see that you won't!"

"You'd better had! You're carrying this hatred of Clara to a point of mania."

He could not altogether deny this, even to himself. His feeling against his father's widow had become a near obsession. And to make it worse, it was fed almost daily by the constant publicity that dogged the footsteps of the famed Mrs. Eric Tyler. The press had its share of lazy reporters, and it was simpler for them, in covering charity balls and tributary dinners, to concentrate on a handful of notables to represent society and whose exits and entrances at caravansaries of pleasure were easily spotted. Clara's graceful figure and designer gowns, her radiant smile for even the most pushing newsman, made her a facile target; her physiognomy had become almost as familiar to the reading public as that of a movie star. And with the record of her foundation spending to counterbalance the luxury of her home life, those same readers could identify with her without any uncomfortable feelings of overprivilege.

It was certainly hard to bear. That the woman who had robbed him of his father, his father's business and his father's wealth should parade before the world not as a shameless adventuress but as a great philanthropist was ample proof, if proof were really needed, that New York society was rotten to the core.

In the revenge that he took upon Clara in his fantasies he saw himself in the role of a Iago, except that his Iago's malignity was far from motiveless. He was not designing a devilish plot against an innocent woman for the exhilaration of playing a life-risking game. No, his Iago would contravene the wicked and expose the unworthy. But there was a hitch, even to fantasy. Shakespeare's Iago was the apparent friend of Desdemona and the intimate of Othello, while Tony was not even on speaking terms with his father's widow.

His only link with her, indeed, was his aunt Elmina, who had always been fonder of him than any of his other relatives, and as she served on the board of the Tyler Foundation and saw its chairman frequently she offered him his only opportunity of keeping an eye on the target of his hostility.

He suggested to Annette that they ask Aunt Elmina for a weekend at their Long Island house.

"Wouldn't a dinner in town do as well?" she counter-proposed. Annette was dutiful about her in-laws, but Miss Tyler for two days and nights was a bit of a task. "What are you trying to get out of the old girl now?"

"Must I always be after something?"

"Well, aren't you?"

He decided that a bit of bait might promote his wife's cooperation. "I want to see if there's any way she can get me on the foundation board. I know she's already proposed it once."

"And what would that get you? Assuming that Clara could ever overcome her aversion."

"The chance to help our favorite charities. Including our girls' school."

"Foundations don't give to private schools."

"They *can*. And they will for a special project if it appeals to them. What about that new library your committee is trying to raise money for?"

He could see that this shaft had gone home. "But I'm afraid you've blotted your copybook fatally with Clara."

"Even if you used all your winning ways on her? You and Aunt Elmina?"

"Don't be silly."

But she was obviously thinking about it. And only two days later she told him that she had given the requested invitation. Miss Tyler would arrive on Friday night in time for dinner.

She not only came; she was in a very expansive and gossipy mood. At dinner with only her nephew and his wife present she talked freely about the foundation's purchase of what she described as an almost sure Ghirlandaio and how cleverly persuasive the curator, Oliver Kip of the Museum of World Art, had been in his interview with the board.

"He and Clara have become quite a team," she concluded with a smirk that seemed to imply a closer intimacy. "I shouldn't be surprised if we bought a number of Italian paintings in the new year. Clara says he's a miracle worker in finding bargains. I wish he'd take *me* to some of his galleries!"

"Is he such a charmer, Auntie?" Annette asked.

"Oh, my dear, he is! Such a high intellectual brow and such courtly manners, even to an old bag like myself. And what an eye! Clara says he can spot a fake, like the princess and the pea, under a dozen mattresses."

Tony's lip curled. "He's really got Clara under his thumb, I take it."

"I don't like to put it that way," his aunt retorted with a sniff. "Clara has exercised her good judgment in his favor. And who's to say she's wrong?"

"Who's to say she's right? The man has bedazzled her, I gather. Is bedazzlement the way to make foundation grants?"

"I think Clara may have what the French call a *faible* for him," Miss Tyler conceded. "But a woman of Clara's intellect and experience can have that for a man without being bedazzled by him."

"Perhaps. But it sounds to me like that old play, *La Ronde*. Where a rich old man is snowed by a designing young woman who, when she grows old herself, is snowed by a young man who's after the fortune she got from the old one."

As soon as he had said this Tony realized his mistake. His aunt was at once indignant. He had given in to the almost irresistible impulse to jeopardize his goal for the pleasure of making one disagreeable remark. Iago would never have been such a fool!

"Clara is hardly an old woman, Tony. And Mr. Kip is almost her age. And she did *not* snow your father!"

"Forgive me, Auntie. It was just an idle crack."

"Well, you should learn not to make such cracks. Particularly in the family. I well realize how bitterly you and Clara have been opposed, but I think it's high time we put all that behind us. Peter Van Alstine has just persuaded her to double the size of the foundation board, which will give her five vacancies to fill. I have been trying to persuade her to put you on, but she has been so reluctant that I decided to postpone my next appeal until the new year. Now, however, with these openings, it seems too good a time to be missed. But it's never going to work if she gets wind of the way you're talking about her."

Tony could have cut his tongue out. But just when he least expected it, an unlikely ally came to his aid.

"That's sweet of you, Auntie," Annette put in. "And I'll do my best to see there are no more 'idle' cracks. At least in my hearing. Do you think it might help if I put in a word to Clara about a changed and repentant Tony? I'm not a bad liar, you know."

Miss Tyler beamed. "I think it would help a lot. She's always liked you, Annette. She might even put you on the board instead of Tony. Though I confess I'd love to see my brother's only son and my father's only grandson a trustee of the Tyler Foundation."

There was nothing for Tony to do after this but bide his time. Time, however, worked in his favor. He didn't even have to protest the odious idea of Annette taking his seat on the coveted board. His aunt's strong preference for blood kin, and the good will that Annette had built up in Clara by her opposition to her husband's lawsuit, produced, in only a few months' time, a letter from his stepmother requesting him to qualify as a trustee. She wrote, coolly but graciously:

"Your aunt has persuaded me that the time has come to bury the hatchet. She believes that your father would have forgiven you for attacking his settlements and that I should do likewise. Because I agree with her about your father's attitude I feel it behooves me to adapt mine to his. Half of the foundation's assets came from your father, and on my death the two halves will be joined. It seems eminently proper that a Tyler son should be represented on the board."

Tony decided that a brief letter indicating only his acceptance and hope for better relations in the future befitted his dignity. At his first meeting with the extended board he remained almost entirely silent. Clara greeted him, as he had anticipated, with a perfect simulacrum of cordiality, even granting him the dividend of one of her lovely open smiles. She was certainly not a grudge bearer, he reflected sourly. But then she had taken all the tricks in the game. So far.

The board met once a month, and it was easy to see, even with its amplified number, that it was essentially the chairman's rubber stamp. Clara presided efficiently and attractively, listening with studied attention to every com-

ment, lauding gracefully the perspicacity of new suggestions, and delivering at last her own preference with clarity, modesty and humor, but nonetheless in a tone that carried with it a certain confidence that it would be adopted,
at least in the case of any major grant. But it was also obvious that she had done her homework on the proposal so
favored and that the objects of her bounty were worthy
ones. And it didn't take Tony long to see that she was very
clever in placating any possible rebels with minor grants
to their pet charities. If he made a pitch for Annette's
school library, he would be sure to draw down something.
But that was not what he was after.

He made a great point of seeking the advice and even
the friendship of the executive director. His excuse for the
lavish lunches at expensive restaurants that he offered the
latter was his need to seek instruction in all the workings
of the foundation, that he might the better perform his
function as a conscientious trustee.

Ignatius Reynolds, a gourmand, wine bibber and gossip, was only too enchanted to be his guest and do his
duty as an instructing executive in this pleasant manner.
"Piggy," as he was unceremoniously known to his inti-
mates, was a stout, moon-faced man of forty-odd years,
with fine, well-pressed cashmere suits draped over his
ample figure and smiles, it seemed, for all. As an art critic
for *Style Magazine* he had written witty and informa-
tive pieces on current urban shows that demonstrated his
considerable acquaintance with contemporary artists and
their different schools. He was amusing and eminently
readable, but his greatest fan would not have accused him
of profundity. Piggy seemed at peace with the world; he

saw no reason to quarrel with any man, woman or creed. There had always to be a way of reconciling oneself to people or causes, no matter how perversely they seemed designed to obstruct one. He was generally supposed, for example, to be gay, but he did nothing openly to affirm or deny it. If he was in the closet, he made no effort to close the door.

The observant Tony, however, spotted other aspects of the man. He was vain about and rigidly tenacious of the social position it had taken him some years to attain. Gotham dinner parties with major Manhattan hostesses were his greatest delight in life. He had little ambition to be anything more than what he contentedly was, but he was always on the watch to see that this status was not diminished by so much as a jot or a tittle. He was, therefore, perfectly satisfied to play second fiddle in foundation matters to the great Clara, who included him regularly in her entertainments, but he was jealous of anyone who designed to exercise a greater influence on his sultana. She must have only one grand vizier, and it didn't take Tony long to see what he could do with *that*.

One day at lunch at Lutèce, after Piggy had finished waving to his friends at other tables, and cocktails had been served, Tony introduced the subject of Oliver Kip. Piggy's warm response was immediate.

"If you want my frank opinion, Tony, I think he's too smooth by half. To the right people, that is. Or to what he considers the right people. To note the difference between the way Mr. Kip greets your stepmother and the way he greets the likes of me is . . . well, awe-inspiring."

"I suppose he feels he has the foundation in his pocket."

"And I'm afraid that to some extent he does. So far, any-way, as we make grants to the Museum of World Art. Of course, he's supposed to have a sharp eye, at least for the Italian Renaissance."

"Supposed to have?"

Piggy hesitated. "Well, I guess I have to concede that when he's operating on his own, in that particular field, he probably makes few mistakes."

Tony moistened his lips in anticipation. "Could you ex-plain what you mean by 'operating on his own'?"

"When he's not being pressed by his trustees or some big shot to acquire a specific object. Or, for example, when he's abroad, and some princess or duchess asks him for the weekend to her historic castle to dispose of a dubious Titian."

"You mean he can be had?"

"Well, let's put it that he can be influenced. He's a terri-ble snob, of course. You'll see that if he ever snubs you. Except he'll never do that, because you're a Tyler."

"Was he operating on his own when he got Clara to pay for the Ghirlandaio?"

"Mmm."

"You don't like the painting? Or you don't like the attri-bution?"

"Oh, I've nothing against the painting. It's very fine. But it's not a Ghirlandaio. And Kip knows it isn't. There's something wrong in the date. He just dreamed up the at-tribution and whispered it to your stepmother to make her think she was putting something over on the gallery. The portrait's a good one — only the foundation paid too much for it."

"How do you know all that?"

"I don't *know* it, Tony. One deduces things. I know the guy at Lecky's who sold the picture. He winked at me after the deal was made and murmured in my ear: 'And now we can expect Mr. Kip to be around to purchase a beautiful little drawing!'"

"You mean as a commission!"

Piggy pretended to look pained. "My dear Tony, must you be so crude? Lecky's can perfectly properly *sell* a drawing to Kip, can it not? And Lecky's can set its own price, can it not? And if Lecky's adjusts that price to reflect a warm, long-standing relationship with a customer who is not only a collector and an expert, but a frequent adviser to the gallery, who can object?"

"It's still most improper!"

"Of course it is. But we must live in this world. I have certainly learned that there are some stones that a foundation director need not go out of his way to turn over."

"You mean you and I should stand by and see the foundation and Clara herself swindled by this guy?"

"She hardly seems to mind!"

"Piggy, suppose she takes it into her head to marry him! How long do you think you'd last at the foundation if he got the least inkling that you know what you know?"

Piggy was now visibly upset. "But he won't! And I don't think she will marry him. And really, Tony, I don't wish to go on with this topic. It's too dangerous!"

"Look, Piggy. With your connections at galleries and museums it should be a simple matter for you to gather enough evidence of Kip's little transactions to blow him out of our picture. All you'd have to do is give it to me, and no one would ever know it came from you. I'd show it to Clara, as something that had been sent to me anonymously, and she'd give Kip his walking papers, so far as she was concerned. Oh, I know her! She can't stand deception!"

"But, Tony, who's going to give me information like that?"

"Almost anyone. Do you think Kip is popular? We know already that he's resented at World Art for grabbing more than his share of the acquisition funds. In the past the big boys at the cultural institutions used to be betrayed by disgruntled secretaries or discharged guards or griping clerks who ransacked their wastepaper baskets. But in our brave new world it's your right-hand man who turns you in, your primary assistant curator, your trusted researcher, who sticks the dagger in your back. After all, who has most to gain from your fall?"

"No, no, it's too risky, much too risky, please, Tony, no more of this!"

Tony knew when to stop; he was learning something about Iago at last. And he knew that he would also know when to pick the matter up again. He even wondered if he would have to, if Piggy, now primed, would not do it for him.

17

CLARA COULD NOT seem to accept gracefully the apparent happiness and fulfillment of her new life. What had she done — or what had she been — to deserve such a fruition of hopes that in the past she had almost fretfully smothered? Nothing, she reminded herself, ever worked out half as well as it was even supposed to. But if by a miracle it did, as now actually seemed to be happening, was it necessary to question one's deserts? Was it ever anything but the blindest luck that one had not been born a leper in darkest Africa or a Jew in the Holocaust? Couldn't she simply lay down her hand and declare a grand slam?

Or at least a small one. She loved her work at the foundation, but she continued to resent Tony's sombre features at the boardroom table. Still, he behaved himself — so far. And Sandra was more of a problem, now that she was a freshman at Barnard. Clara was surprised that she had not gone farther afield for college to free herself from living at home, but apparently there was a young man who kept her in town (she was not communicative about this) and then, too, she belonged to a very active local women's lib group. Sandra was not argumentative, like so many of her contemporaries, nor did she seem eager to convert her mother to her causes; it was really rather worse than that. She seemed to regard Clara as material too unpromising, as someone whose day has passed and who should be treated with benign neglect.

But none of that was really the point. Of course, it wasn't! Why, Clara demanded of her lineless image in the morning mirror as she rubbed powder into her cheeks, was she always shying away from her principal concern. *When* should she make a probing analysis of her relationship with Oliver? It was only perfect, she kept telling herself, because she wanted so desperately to have it perfect. She went to his apartment every Wednesday and Saturday afternoon — he was nothing if not methodical — where they made love rapturously but briefly. He continued to enjoy sketching her in the nude. They would chatter and laugh together about all kinds of subjects — except love. He was always delightful but never really serious. Except, of course, about Italian art.

At last, however, she had put the question to him. After all, she *was* a woman.

"Tell me something, Oliver. Have you ever loved anyone? And I don't mean your mother."

"As a matter of fact, I *didn't* really love my mother. Our relationship was more like Agrippina and Nero."

"And what is ours?"

Oliver shook his head as if stumped. Then he seemed to pass his case to Shelley: "I can give not what men call love, / But wilt thou accept not / The worship the heart lifts above / And the heavens reject not?"

Clara had to smile. She had almost expected it! "The desire of the moth for the star?"

He nodded. "And the night for the morrow."

"No way!" she retorted with a laugh. "Shelley was a monstrous betrayer who tried to cover it up with lovely lines. But who but fools were fooled?"

"I see you may be that rare woman, Clara, who can take what life offers and not spoil it, like Oliver Twist, by asking for more."

"Is *that* why you never married?"

He was almost grave for once. "And never shall."

She turned her face away. She was afraid he might make out a shade of disappointment. Was it true, after all, that she was like all his other women, whoever they had been? But if he suspected any such reaction he did not show it. He seemed to be offering her what to his mind was surely the greatest compliment of all: that of assuming that she was as highly civilized as himself.

"My life is not the kind that can be improved by being shared," he went on to explain. "And I'm not such a clumsy ass as to seek a role that wouldn't become me."

So there it was. She had suspected it; she had sought it, and she had got it! And she was going to live with it, if it killed her.

"Do you know something?" she asked. "I got your birthday from your secretary. And it's next Saturday! Let us go gallery-vanting for a master drawing!"

Ah, the glitter in his eyes was almost worth it!

"And will you pick one out for me?"

"Do you think I'm such a fool? No, you'll do that, of course. My fun will be in watching you do it."

The next Saturday morning, before she set out to meet him, she had breakfast with Sandra.

"Will you be in for lunch?" she asked her. "Oliver's coming. He might be able to help you with some fine points on your paper on Machiavelli in modern world politics."

"But Oliver hates silly questions from amateurs."

"Your questions wouldn't be silly, dear."

"He might make me feel they were."

"Oliver? His manners are perfect."

"But I can see they're manners."

Clara looked at her daughter more closely now. "You don't really like Oliver, do you?"

"Does it matter? He's not *my* friend."

"No, but he's mine. And if my daughter dislikes him, it interests me to know why."

Sandra appeared to be debating the justice of this inquiry. But at last she nodded affirmatively. "Very well. He strikes me as a man for whom other people don't really exist. In any important way, that is. I may be going too far. Some great art critic might exist for him. A Berenson, say."

"He thinks Berenson's greatly overrated."

"Well, there you are. I suspect he thinks everyone's overrated. Except Oliver Kip. And there's something else about him that I don't buy. I'm sure he doesn't think women play any great role in art."

"Well, they didn't in the Renaissance."

"Just Lucrezia Borgias, is that it? Ladies with whom it was not quite safe to dine?"

"I hope he doesn't think that of me!"

"Oh, no, Mom, you're his Isabella d'Este. But even she comes a long way after the least male artist or despot of the Renaissance."

"Darling, do you ever think that your passionate espousal of women's lib may carry you a bit to extremes?"

"Not as much as your disdain of it blinds you to some important facts."

Clara saw now that they were going to be serious, perhaps more than she strictly needed. But there had not been so many opportunities, and she decided to take this one. "I should really appreciate it, my dear, if you would tell me what those facts are."

There was another pause before Sandra's decisive nod seemed again to clear the air. "All right. Here goes. Your being put on the board of Riker's Oil and Gas. And of Western Air. You think that's such a stride in the recognition of women?"

"And it isn't?"

"It might have been if what the companies were seeking was a woman who could help them in their business. But they weren't. What they wanted was a shining token of their boasted freedom from gender bias. A beautiful great lady with a name famous in fashion. A showpiece! And they got one!"

Clara gripped the edge of the table. A blow from a child was always unnerving. "I suppose you think my whole life has been like that."

"Oh, Mother, I'm not judging you!"

"Are you not?"

"No! It's not your fault. You belong to the last generation of women who have been brought up to use their sex appeal to further their ambition."

"I see. I'm glad, anyway, you admit I had it. And your generation, they disdain all that, I suppose. They don't care if they're wall-eyed or hunchbacks?"

"No, it's not that. People are always going to play a trump card if they think they have one. What I mean is that a serious professional woman today, in becoming a leader in law or medicine or business, regards her charm or glamor or whatever you call it, and if she has any, as something belonging to an entirely different department from her brains and drive. And to be used for entirely different purposes. Just as men do."

"Whereas my poor contemporaries mixed them all up?"

"Something like that."

"You really think we're just courtesans, isn't that it?"

"Mother, you're going much too far."

"And tell me this. You think I married your father and Eric for their money?"

Sandra looked as if she were about to repudiate this, but she suddenly closed her lips. "Would you have married either of them had he been poor?"

"No!" Clara rose at this. "Enough of this. Now go to your class or your meeting or whatever you're going to!"

It was a relief to get out of the house and into a cold morning, and she walked all the way to her appointment with Oliver on Madison Avenue. They visited four different galleries in two crowded hours before he took her to a shop specializing in baroque drawings of the seventeenth century, a period rather later than Oliver's favorite, but she had learned that he was extending his taste to include stage designs. And when he drew out of a folio one by Andrea Pozzo she could tell by his reverent handling of it that they were looking at his birthday gift.

It was the sketch for the backdrop of a scene in ancient Rome of a tragedy or opera, showing a magnificent imperial stairwell winding up and upwards to seeming infinity and, towering over it, a glorious architectural fantasy of arches, domes, cupolas, pediments and myriad tall columns, while teeming all over the steps were the tiny togaed figures of the citizens who ruled the world.

"Of course, I see why you like it so," she told him.

"Meaning that you don't?"

"Oh, I admire it. Who wouldn't? It's a dazzling thing. But I don't agree with it. It says that art is all and people are nothing. Happy birthday, dear Oliver! Shall I tell them to wrap and send, or will you take it with you?"

"Do you think I'll let it out of my sight?"

He was so eager to get home with his treasure that she rescinded her invitation to lunch, which turned out to be just as well, for when she came through her own front door she found Polly Madison in the hall taking off her hat.

"I hope you can stay for lunch," she addressed her cheerfully. "Otherwise I'll be all alone. Oliver's left me for a new mistress!"

But when Polly turned, Clara was faced with features quite unprepared for jest. "What do you mean by *that*?"

"Oh, only that he's in love with a drawing I gave him for his birthday."

Polly's eyes widened. "Which is precisely what I've come to talk to you about. Never mind lunch. For a bit anyway. Give me a drink. And yourself one. You're going to need it."

In the living room, before the needed tray and ice,

Clara sat and listened to what her friend had to say. She found herself curiously unsurprised.

Miss Tyler, it appeared, had garnered the story from her nephew and brought it to Polly as the only person who could properly break it to Clara. Tony had received convincing information from an undisclosed source that Oliver Kip had, on each of the four occasions when the Tyler Foundation had made grants to the Museum of World Art for the purchase of paintings recommended by him, received a master drawing from the dealer selling the painting.

"Received?" Clara asked. "How do you know he didn't pay a full price for them? He's a known collector, you know, and he buys all over town."

"Oh, we're sure he paid *something*. It would have been folly not to. But Tony's informant suggests that the prices were nominal."

"And what, assuming all this to be true, does Auntie want me to do about it?"

"She hopes, of course, that you will break off with Kip."

"And if I don't?"

"Then she's afraid that Tony will seek to have the board replace you as chairman."

"With himself as my replacement?"

"Well, his position would be that you are not fit for the job so long as you are subject to undue influence."

"He's tried that undue influence business before. Without much success, as we all remember."

"Oh, Clara, do be careful!"

"I'm going to be very careful, I promise you, dear."

"What will you do?"

"Well, I think the first thing will be to have a little chat with Mr. Kip, don't you?"

<hr/>

Oliver sat in an armchair before the easel on which her birthday gift was exhibited. He contemplated it in the silence that followed her disclosure to which he had listened without comment or change of expression. The only thing that struck her as different from his normal composure was that he now reached for a cigarette and lighted it.

"That my purchases — and purchases they were — coincided with the museum's could be a coincidence."

"Of course, they could," she agreed hastily. "And I'm not suggesting they weren't. But it could be made to look like a pattern."

"And will be, no doubt, by those who want to see me hanged. Oh, yes, I could well lose my job. The trustees would zap me on a suspicion; they don't need anything as prosaic as truth. But so what? World Art isn't the only museum in creation. My mail contains some pretty tempting offers."

"But would they continue if word got out why World Art let you go?"

He shrugged. "It might be a bit sticky for a while. At least on this side of the Atlantic. But Europeans are less puritan. In fact, there's an institution in Rome where I might be even happier than here."

"There's still something you can do that will stop your opponents dead in their tracks."

"And what, pray, is that, my dear?"

Clara fixed her eyes on him steadily before she spoke. "Make a public announcement that the propriety of your four purchases of master drawings has been questioned. Assert strongly that they were arm's-length transactions, the results of close bargaining. And then conclude with the statement that, to avoid even a scintilla of doubt, you are giving the four drawings to World Art."

Oliver looked at her blankly. "You are very generous with other people's property. Those four drawings are the pearls of my collection."

"Which is just why my idea will succeed!"

He shook his head. "Never! I won't do it!"

She viewed him with amazement. He *was*, after all, the man she had thought him. The man? Well, whatever it was, he was it. Her heart seemed to turn into quartz as she reached for the card she had hoped she wouldn't have to play.

"There is something else that may persuade you. Something that I saw in your eyes when we were looking at *that* in the gallery this morning." She pointed to the Pozzo. "It was something even stronger than what you feel for any item in your collection. It was the desire to *acquire* an item. The collector's passion! It's like a sexual drive. Much more potent than any love for the baby produced."

"That's a rather crude way of putting it. But who's to say you don't have a point?"

"Not you, anyway. What I offer you, Oliver, is this: give the drawings to the museum, and I'll pay you for them. At their current market value."

"Clara, that will cost you a fat sum! Think of it!"

"I'd rather think of all the pleasure you will have spending it at auction galleries!"

"But if it should ever get out —"

"It won't get out. I'll pay you over a period. And into Swiss accounts! Will you do it, Oliver?"

"Oh, you know I'll do it. We might even have a drink over it." He rose and went to his pantry from which she heard the pop of a champagne cork. He returned with the bottle and two glasses on a silver tray. He raised his solemnly.

"To the end of our ever interesting affair."

"Oliver! What makes you say that?"

"Well, it's so, isn't it? Hadn't you decided, before you came today, that if I agreed to take your money it would be over between us? Oh, I don't mean our friendship necessarily. We're both intelligent enough to enjoy that. But what the tabloids would call our fling, our walk-out."

"Mightn't they even call it our romance?"

"At any rate, we know what we're talking about. And we both know it's over."

"You're not taking the money to be rid of me?"

"I'm taking the money, my love, because I want the money. It's as simple as that. And I'm always willing to pay the price."

"Isn't that rather begging the question?"

Which enabled them to end a difficult interview with a laugh. Clara put down her glass and almost fled from his apartment. The details of their pact could be worked out later.

She walked rapidly the long blocks home. She knew now that she would survive the break. For what had she not survived? The museum would be silenced by its splendid acquisitions; Tony would be left, as the saying was, with egg on his face; she would be stronger than ever as the foundation chairman; there would be no stain on the radiant persona of Clarabel Tyler. And she might even have bought off a jealous and puritan God by her self-punishment in the cost to her income of her deal with Oliver! Perhaps Sandra was wrong about there being no place for Madame de Pompadour in the age of computers.

At any rate, it was too late for her to change.

18

THE BRIEF KIP SCANDAL blew away entirely with Oliver's gift of the four drawings, including "Christ Finding the Apostles Asleep," to the Museum of World Art, and their gracious acceptance by the trustees of that institution, and Tony Tyler, presumably relieved that his stepmother had not sought other reprisal, abandoned his plots against the chairman. Or if he didn't, Clara at least heard of none. She never vouchsafed a word on the matter to him and even accorded him a minor grant for his children's school library. She knew the dangers of being a vindictive victor.

She invited Oliver to her bigger dinner parties, and he made himself as agreeable a guest as ever, but she never again worked directly with him over a proposed purchase for his museum, confining herself to the consideration of applications from World Art prepared by the Acquisitions Committee. The reputation of the foundation for judicious and imaginative giving continued to grow, and a large percentage of it was attributed to its active and hardworking chairman.

In the presidential campaign of 1960 Clara contributed heavily from her own funds to promote the election of Senator Kennedy, and after his inauguration rumors reached her from Washington that her name was under consideration for the ambassadorship to the Caribbean island republic of Santa Emilia, a small enough nation, to be sure, but one containing a benign climate, a lush vegetation and a famous winter beach resort, Puerta Castilia.

The first person, however, with whom she discussed the advisability of accepting the post was not enthusiastic. Sandra, who had now moved into the apartment of her boy friend, called early one morning to bring her Grant Lucas's point of view.

"To begin with, Grant is not overly enthusiastic about this whole new Kennedy regime."

"But he voted for him, didn't he?"

"There was no alternative. But he's very dubious about the crowd around Kennedy. They're too rich and bright and handsome and full of themselves. They're the image of idealism rather than idealism itself. Grant says Americans only care for something that *looks* like the real thing. That's what movies and TV have done to us. People actually prefer looks to reality. Or maybe they hope that looks *are* reality!"

Clara found her daughter's boy friend the most tedious type of liberal: the dry economist (he wrote a column for a leftist sheet) who can never be satisfied with any party so long as he can poke a hole in its program. It irritated her that Sandra should submit her better mind to his.

"Sometimes we have to make do with what we've got. And anyway, what has that to do with Santa Emilia?"

"Well, don't you see, Ma, the job Kennedy's offering you is just looks all over again? He's rewarding your cash contribution with a free vacation spot, where you can entertain all your friends and have the titillating title of Mrs. Ambassador! Diplomacy these days is conducted on the telephone between the chief of state and the president, and if anything more is required the secretary of state flies in!"

"And I'll be there to receive him! And how do you know I won't be perfectly happy just to have people address me as Mrs. Ambassador?"

"Oh, Ma, if you're going to make a joke of the whole thing there's no point talking to you."

But Clara had found their little chat more painful than she cared to admit. There was a kind of musical comedy aspect to the rumored appointment, and it seemed to cast an ironic aura over her whole life. Had anyone ever taken her seriously? Did it even matter what grants her foundation made? Wasn't it bound to make them anyway, and wouldn't any half-rational board of trustees do about as well as any other? The needs were endless; anywhere the money went, it would do *some* good.

Polly was better company in her crisis. Stuart was now doing a tour of duty in the State Department, and he had some views on Santa Emilia which he had authorized his wife to impart to her friend. Clara took her out to lunch on the same day that Sandra had called.

"In the first place," Polly announced after they were seated at their table, "the rumor is true. You *are* going to be offered the post. In the second place, Stuart is not at all sure that you should accept it. Of course, this is between us. It wouldn't do for Stuart to be known to have counseled anyone to decline a presidential appointment."

"Of course. And you can be sure it will never be known through me."

"He knows you're my best friend. He wouldn't do this for anyone." Polly paused to let this sink in. And Clara did recognize that from such a bureaucrat as Stuart this was indeed a signal favor. Perhaps one day he would need one from a foundation. God, did she have to suspect *everybody?*

"Stuart has a lot of Caribbean friends from his old Panama days," Polly continued now. "And one in particular who does a lot of business in Santa Emilia. He maintains there's a lot more going on there than the CIA is aware of. Of course, Stuart, like most State Department regulars, has no great love for the CIA. He thinks they're neglecting too many spots in the Caribbean in their obsession with Cuba. He thinks they may push us into a mess with Cuba."

"Well, Cuba's a long way from Santa Emilia. I don't know much about Santa Emilia, but I can read a map."

"That's not Stuart's point, dear. His point is that his friend thinks the radicals in Santa Emilia, the so-called People's Party, are much stronger than generally believed. He says they're ready for a coup."

Clara's body froze in immediate attention and excitement. "A coup that will succeed?"

"Who knows? But a coup that will be a blood bath! Stuart thinks you should use all your charm on Kennedy and hold out for Luxembourg. There you could be an overnight success!"

"But can't you see, Polly, that's not what I want? I've had all that!"

"You prefer a blood bath?"

"Much! I look my best in red crepe de chine!"

Polly sniffed. "It's a pity so many have to die to deck you out."

"But they're not going to die for me! *I'm* certainly not causing their deaths. Oh, I know, it may sound ruthless of me to take advantage of disaster, but can't you and I be frank? How else are names made in this world? What would George Washington have been without George III? A surveyor! What would Churchill have been without Hitler? The bungler of Gallipoli! Don't stand between me and my one chance, Polly!"

"Your one chance? My God, if I'd had a fraction of what you've had, my gal! Why can't you rest on your laurels, marry some decent gent and settle down to a life of serene middle age? You have your foundation, isn't that enough?"

"I don't want any more men in my life. Not just now, anyway. I haven't been good with men. Sandra says I've been all mixed up between playing the siren and trying to be a modern female."

"Sandra says that? She has a nerve."

"Well, she thinks it anyway, and to some extent she's right. I was more of a mistress than a wife to Trevor. Maybe that was partly his fault. And I was more of a daughter than a lover to Eric. That was certainly more than partly his fault. And to Oliver, what was I trying to be? A mother? If so, I succeeded, for I had no influence on him at all. Well, what the hell? Now I'm going to be myself."

"And what is that, dear friend?"

"An ambassador!"

"God bless you, anyway. And good luck!"

When Clara returned to her house after lunch, she heard the telephone ringing, and she picked it up in the hall. It was the president!

"Hello, Clara! You probably know what I'm calling about. Everyone here seems to know what I'm doing before I do."

"You want me to be ambassador to Santa Emilia."

"That's it! How about it?"

"Oh, I accept, with gratitude, Mr. President."

"Great! Have you ever been there?"

"No. But I managed to find it on the map."

"Don't be picky. Size isn't everything. I'm told it has a wonderful beach. At Puerta Castilia. Perhaps Jackie and I will join you on a vacation there."

"I'll have it ready. I might even arrange a revolution for you."

"Why do you say that? Do you know something I don't know? It wouldn't be surprising."

"No. It's just that those people are always having revolutions, aren't they? And if they do, please don't send the secretary of state. Let me handle it myself, will you?"

"Clara, you've been on my team for exactly two minutes, and you're already giving me orders. Is it going to be that way with every woman I appoint?"

"You should be so lucky, Mr. President."

"Well, come to see me and Jackie before you go. She sends her love."

"And mine to her."

Clara solemnly kissed the telephone after she hung up.

223

Then she turned her mind to her preparations. She would take Annie Hally with her as her secretary. Peter Van Alstine could take her place as foundation chairman in her absence. If, in his opinion, Tony should ever show enough maturity and development to take over that job, it should be considered. And she would write her mother to remind her of Oscar Wilde's dictum that children start by loving their parents. Later, they judge them. Rarely if ever do they forgive them. Well, she forgave Violet. She forgave her utterly.